Royal Christmas at Seattle General

A very royal Christmas surprise awaits…

As trees go up, snow begins to fall, lights begin to sparkle and gifts are wrapped, the esteemed Seattle General Hospital Emergency Room team prepares for a festive season they won't soon forget!

Head ER doc Domenico di Rossi has long kept his identity as Crown Prince of Isola Verde a secret, so when his father is admitted to the ER, chaos erupts and unexpected Christmas miracles are set in motion for everyone in the hospital. Now, with lives on the line, secrets to hide, a throne to be claimed, and hearts to win and lose, it's clear that this Christmas will be the most dramatic yet for the team at Seattle General Hospital!

Available now:

Falling for the Secret Prince
by Alison Roberts

Neurosurgeon's Christmas to Remember
by Traci Douglass

The Bodyguard's Christmas Proposal
by Charlotte Hawkes

The Princess's Christmas Baby
by Louisa George

Dear Reader,

I loved writing this book for the Royal Christmas at Seattle General series! I got to work with some awesome authors and we had such fun brainstorming glamorous settings, beautiful ball gowns and menu ideas for a Christmas ball.

Princess Gigi and Dr. Lucas Beaufort hadn't planned on being together in the lead-up to Christmas, or any time at all after their brief fling in August. But fate (and this mean author!) had other ideas…

Sure, their summer liaison had been hot and intense, but neither of them believed a relationship between a princess who lived on a beautiful Mediterranean island and a trauma consultant halfway across the world in Seattle could be possible. There were too many obstacles. Too many reasons why not…

But add in a little complication and they had to find ways to compromise. Soon the sparks were flying again!

I really hope you enjoy *The Princess's Christmas Baby* as much as I did writing it. I love hearing from readers, so please do get in touch either via my website, www.louisageorge.com, where you can sign up for all my release news, or on Facebook, louisageorgebooks.

Happy reading!

Louisa x

THE PRINCESS'S CHRISTMAS BABY

———

LOUISA GEORGE

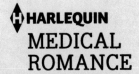

HARLEQUIN

MEDICAL
ROMANCE

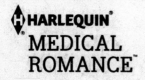

HARLEQUIN®
MEDICAL
ROMANCE™

Recycling programs
for this product may
not exist in your area.

ISBN-13: 978-1-335-14980-0

The Princess's Christmas Baby

Copyright © 2020 by Harlequin Books S.A.

All rights reserved. No part of this book may be used or reproduced in
any manner whatsoever without written permission except in the case of
brief quotations embodied in critical articles and reviews.

This is a work of fiction. Names, characters, places and incidents
are either the product of the author's imagination or are used fictitiously.
Any resemblance to actual persons, living or dead, businesses,
companies, events or locales is entirely coincidental.

This edition published by arrangement with Harlequin Books S.A.

For questions and comments about the quality of this book,
please contact us at CustomerService@Harlequin.com.

Harlequin Enterprises ULC
22 Adelaide St. West, 40th Floor
Toronto, Ontario M5H 4E3, Canada
www.Harlequin.com

Printed in U.S.A.

Award-winning author **Louisa George** has been an avid reader her whole life. In between chapters, she's managed to train as a nurse, marry her doctor hero and have two sons. Now she writes chapters of her own in the medical romance, contemporary romance and women's fiction genres. Louisa's books have variously been nominated for the coveted RITA® Award and the New Zealand Koru Award and have been translated into twelve languages. She lives in Auckland, New Zealand.

Books by Louisa George

Harlequin Medical Romance

SOS Docs
Saved by Their One-Night Baby

The Ultimate Christmas Gift
The Nurse's Special Delivery

The Hollywood Hills Clinic
Tempted by Hollywood's Top Doc

Midwives On-Call at Christmas
Her Doctor's Christmas Proposal

200 Harley Street: The Shameless Maverick
A Baby on Her Christmas List
Tempted by Her Italian Surgeon
Reunited by Their Secret Son
A Nurse to Heal His Heart
A Puppy and a Christmas Proposal

Visit the Author Profile page
at Harlequin.com for more titles.

PROLOGUE

August

IT WAS HIS idea of hell.

When Lucas Beaufort had said to his best friend Domenico that if he ever needed any help with anything, just ask, he hadn't meant he'd be free at the drop of a hat to babysit his friend's reckless younger sister who made the papers for all the wrong reasons.

But there it was. Sometimes friendships required going above and beyond. He only hoped he'd manage to get through this weekend unscathed.

Which he highly doubted. Take one wilful and wayward, spoilt Princess...with a capital P. Literally. Add her ability to make trouble for herself wherever she went. Sprinkle in a rogue weekend in Seattle during which she was expecting to be entertained, and he knew—even though his cooking was generally woeful—that he had a recipe for utter disaster on his hands.

'Hey, Captain Sensible!' She flung herself at him as he opened the door to her loud hammering. 'Long time no see.'

'About ten years, give or take.' And he'd hoped for longer, but there it was. He tried to extricate himself from her hug but she kind of held on. Captain Sensible, eh? Great. He guessed he probably deserved it. He wasn't exactly known for his witty repartee. 'Come in, Giada. Welcome back to Seattle.'

She finally let go and grinned as he took a step outside to grab her suitcase and let her into his house. As they walked through to his living room she flung her floppy sunhat onto his sofa and slipped off her over-sized sunglasses. She was wearing a strappy, white sundress and…well, hell. She'd changed since he'd seen her last.

Whereas years ago she'd gone through a typical but lengthy rebellious, pale-skinned goth phase, with ripped jeans and black clothes totally unbefitting a royal, she was now a picture of glowing health—all tanned arms and legs with long shiny black hair that cascaded in waves over her shoulders. Her dark brown eyes glittered as she smiled and made him want to take a second look. Her mouth.

God…it was very bad that he was looking at his best friend's sister's mouth.

She also smelled exactly how he imagined her

home, the Mediterranean island of Isola Verde, would smell: fresh, flowery, warm. Weird that he'd even notice.

'Well, this is nice,' she said as she ran to the huge picture window and took in the expansive view over Lake Washington. Her voice was singsong and…happy. Which made him feel immediately wistful. Happy. Yeah. Half turning, she twisted to look at him. 'No, not nice. It's gorgeous here, Lucas. Thanks for putting me up… I mean…' she laughed and made quote marks with her fingers '…*putting up with me* for the weekend.'

'It's not a problem.' Although, judging by the fact he'd noticed her perfume and was taking another look at her pretty face, it could well turn into a problem. She was so off limits it wasn't funny.

'I promise I'll be on my best behaviour, Lucas. Too bad Dom has to spend the weekend at some dull conference instead of showing his sister around the city he prefers to his beautiful island home.' She whirled round to face him fully, her dress flaring out around her thighs.

Lucas looked. So sue him. 'It's fine. Um… What would you like to do?'

'Swim first? Or a shower. But I'd prefer a swim if I can, just to have a good workout and stretch. I really need to freshen up after that flight.'

'Sure thing. Lake or pool?'

'Lake. There's nothing better than swimming in nature, right? It reminds me of home.' She let out a big sigh. A sigh he couldn't read. 'Oh, and call me Gigi. Everyone else does. You want to come for a dip?'

He couldn't remember the last time he'd swum in the lake. Just the usual fifty laps of his pool each morning. Clinical. Routine.

The thought of his feet sinking into warm sand was definitely appealing. As was seeing more of those long shapely legs. She was a lot more attractive than he remembered. Softer too…none of that spiky aggression he remembered. None of the artifice, the heavy make-up she used to hide behind.

No…she wasn't pretty, she was stunning. He was not going to think of her in a bathing suit. Or, *God*…a bikini. His body prickled in response.

So basically he needed a cold shower, not a swim with her. 'I have work to do. The lake is at the end of the garden. It's safe for swimming and the little beach is very private so you won't be disturbed. When you get back we can make a plan for the rest of the weekend.'

'Oh, come on, Lucas. It's after six. You should have clocked off by now.' She brushed against him as she breezed over to her suitcase and he felt the hairs on his arm stand to attention. 'Surely you can spare an hour for a swim? Dom tells me you work too hard.'

'You don't get to be an emergency consultant by taking time off whenever you feel like it. Or by endless partying.' Or getting onto the front pages by being drunk and messy on some celebrity's yacht. Or crashing the stage at festivals. He decided not to mention her past antics, though; she'd clearly changed. Outwardly, anyway.

'Ouch.' She laughed. 'I take it that was a jab at me and my sorry life to date?'

'No.' He wasn't going to add to the mess he was starting to make here.

'Well, I'm grateful you've taken this weekend off for me. Really, I am.' Despite his unforgivably negative tone her smile was warm and did something to his gut. 'But it's fine. Stay here and do your work. Maybe we could go out for a meal or something later. I'd like to pick your brains about the Isola Verde hospital project I'm working on. If you have the time.'

Where was the flake he had known? 'What hospital project?'

'You're busy. Honestly, it can wait. But the swim can't. I'm too hot and sticky to think straight. I'll go get changed.' She picked up her bag, shoulders sagging just a little. 'Which room should I use?'

'I'll show you.' He was drawn back to look at

her eyes. Wide and dark and deep with an understanding, a knowledge of difficult times. Of pride too. And now they glittered as she smiled and he got a glimpse of the old rebellious Giada. But she was much more than the ditzy party girl she had once been. He took her bag and walked her through to the guest room. 'And you'll be okay at the lake?'

She nodded. 'Absolutely. No problem. I'm quite used to entertaining myself.'

Her smile might have been warm but she blinked too fast and he just knew she was pretending to be fine when she wasn't.

'You head on down. I'll just be five minutes and then I'll join you.'

The smile of gratitude she gave him made his gut do somersaults. Which should have been enough warning.

And he should have listened.

Gigi hadn't remembered Lucas being so grumpy. Or so gorgeous. Maybe she hadn't been looking too closely all those years ago when she'd met him at some dull hospital party, and she certainly hadn't been interested in any of her brother's boring friends, choosing to find her own entertainment elsewhere.

But Lucas Beaufort was next level stunning with his dark blond hair and piercing green eyes.

Just wow. And just her luck he was her brother's best friend and therefore totally and utterly out of bounds.

And now she was stuck with him for three days.

The water was soothing and coolly refreshing. She thrashed through her strokes until she was breathless and her limbs sore. Exercise had become her salve instead of the partying she'd once used to escape her life.

Take that, Captain Sensible. People changed.

He hadn't directly mentioned her past, but she was familiar with the look of judgement. Hell, she'd had it every single day of her life from her papa. She hoped Lucas didn't put her in the same box everyone else did, but it was a badge she'd earned many times over.

She was different now. If only people could believe it.

Tired, but definitely less stressed, she trod water, turning in a slow circle to take in the view of the city's high rises in one direction, the endless horizon in another, Denny-Blaine Park and... *Oddio!*

Lucas wasn't just gorgeous, he was a freaking hunk on legs, wading into the water towards her, not quite deep enough for his muscular thighs to be submerged. She traced up with her eyes...then swallowed. *My, oh, my.*

What was under those aqua-blue shorts?

She dragged her gaze higher, past the hard wall of a six, no…an eight pack, past broad shoulders to his proud jaw and unsmiling mouth.

She watched as he dived through the gentle waves and swam towards her with fast, easy strokes.

He is not hot. He is not hot.

Lucas rose up in front of her, flicking water from his hair. Little droplets clung to his impossibly long eyelashes, framing searching green eyes.

'You okay, Giada? It's quite deep out here.'

She'd forgotten he was English before she'd arrived, although his accent was very definitely infused with a Pacific Northwest twang since he'd been here almost as long as Dom had. 'It's Gigi. Yes. I'm fine. Isola Verde is an island, I swim a lot.'

'All the same, maybe we should go where it's shallower.' He stretched his arms out and her gaze was drawn to the toned biceps. The sprinkling of hair on his tanned chest. The stubble on his jaw. Those serious eyes.

What would it take to make him smile? How would he look if he did? And why did she want him to? She was only here for a couple of days and then she'd be back home, overseeing the final touches to her beloved hospital. Trying to be a better person.

Admiring a man's body was all well and good but it wasn't as if she could take anything any further. Especially not with Lucas. Brother's best friend. Inhabitant of Seattle…thousands of miles away from Isola Verde where her future lay. Her papa had always told her she dated unsuitable men and that she should set her sights on someone from one of the European royal families.

Boring.

She stole another look at this unsuitable man's broad shoulders, those full, kissable lips, that little trail of dark hair arrowing down to his shorts. Her imagination caught her low in her belly.

Just how sensible would Captain Sensible be in bed?

She dived under the water and tried to use the bracing cold to wash the very inappropriate and surprisingly sexy thoughts from her brain. Which was a mistake. Because down here she could see his legs, the ripples of his belly, his shorts…

When she broke the surface again he was frowning. 'You were down there so long I thought you were drowning or something.'

She laughed. 'I like to live dangerously.'

'So I've heard.' Of course he had. Everyone knew everything about her. Or almost, at least. He shook his head, clearly unimpressed. 'Can you imagine what Dom would do to me if I allowed you to get into trouble out here?'

'Depends on the trouble.' She laughed again, mischievously, watching the double meaning sink into his brain and the shock register in his eyes. Okay, so maybe she hadn't quite mastered *all* her spontaneity. And the cold water treatment clearly hadn't worked.

He twisted in the water, sending an arc of droplets into the air. They caught the fading light, a dozen fleeting rainbows haloing him. 'It's getting late and it's going to be dark soon. We should get out.'

'Okay, Captain. Race you to the beach.' She dived deep then, not waiting around for his reaction. When she surfaced she saw him powering ahead of her.

She dug deep and swung her arms into action and they hit the shallows at the same time. She stood up and kicked a swash of water into an arc towards him. 'Wow. You're good, Lucas.'

He looked at her, eyes dark, and she thought for a moment he was going to growl but, surprisingly, he kicked and splashed water over her. She shrieked and kicked back, following him to the water's edge and drenching him again.

'Hey. Mind the food!' he shouted, the glimpse of playfulness melting away as he pointed to the little grassy bank, where he'd left a rug and a picnic basket.

She hadn't realised she was hungry, but the

thought of food made her stomach rumble. 'You brought a picnic?'

He ran and grabbed a towel from a pile by the basket and started to rub himself dry. 'Thought you might be hungry.'

'You're a proper adult, Lucas Beaufort. Thank you.'

After throwing the towel back on the grass, he reached into the basket and took out a bottle of fizzy water and two glasses. 'Honestly? I was starving.'

'Typical man, always thinking about food.'

'I had my housekeeper make it up for us.' He poured water into the glasses and handed one to her. 'Wasn't sure what a princess likes to snack on so there's plenty of everything.'

'I'm just a normal woman, Lucas. I eat anything and everything. But particularly...' She peered into the basket to discover olives and cheese and sourdough bread. 'Oh, this looks perfect. Just like my favourite Isola Verde treats. Did you know we have the best olives and tomatoes in the Mediterranean?'

'I think Dom has mentioned it once or a million times.'

'And our wine's amazing.' She sat on the rug, rubbed her damp body with a towel then wrapped it around her shoulders. 'Our grapes are perfect for dessert wine, which is delicious. Although some would say I've drunk far more than my fair share over the years.'

'Don't do that, Giada.' His tone was sharp.

She whipped round to look at him. 'What?'

'Don't put yourself down. We all did stupid things when we were young.'

'Oh, Captain Sensible, I saw you at that Medics Ball ten years ago. You were the epitome of good manners and here you are now looking after a princess in the nicest, safest way possible. There isn't even wine for us to get silly on. I can't imagine you doing anything you'd regret.'

'I've done plenty.'

'Oh?' It looked like the captain was about to share.

He shook his head. Maybe not.

She turned onto her belly, brushing his arm, gooseflesh rising at that fleeting skin-to-skin contact. It was strange, but this secluded magical place felt deeply intimate. 'Come on, Lucas. What do you regret? I bet it wasn't barfing down the side of an A-list film star's yacht in front of the world's media at the Naples Film Festival?'

His eyebrows rose. 'No. But I did see those pictures.'

'Ugh.' She shuddered at the memory. 'You and everyone else. Nothing can be as bad as that, right? Come on, what do you regret?'

He shrugged, opened his mouth then closed it

again. There was something, but he clearly wasn't going to bare his soul to a relative stranger. Then he said, 'Entering a chilli-eating contest. It was for charity but even so…that was definitely not a good idea. Especially when you have work the next morning.' He snagged her gaze and she had the feeling he was on the edge of a smile.

What was he holding back?

She laughed, bewitched by the different hues in his irises—amber, gold and green. 'Can't say I'm a chilli fan.'

'And you should probably stay that way. But I couldn't back down because it was being streamed live on the internet for people to watch and pay however much they thought my pain was worth. You're not allowed to drink water or anything to help cool your mouth. I had tears running down my face, lips on fire, with a couple of thousand people enjoying my pain in real time. Your brother was the worst, egging me on from the sidelines.'

He almost smiled as he talked but didn't quite manage it. Giada breathed out, realising she'd been waiting to see the glow of joy or happiness or just plain fun emanating from him. But, even though he'd lightened up, she couldn't describe him as relaxed.

'I never even heard about that.' Though it was hardly surprising given she and Dom didn't always share details of their days or even weeks sometimes.

'Trust me, it wasn't pretty. I had my one taste of fame and I hated it. Honestly, Giada, I don't know how you can live under the glare of such scrutiny.'

She shrugged. 'I'd like to say I'm never in embarrassing situations, but that wouldn't be true. You do get used to the cameras.'

'I would never get used to them.'

A cool breeze fanned over her, making her shiver, and Lucas seemed to notice because he wrapped her towel more tightly around her shoulders. The action was so tender it made her heart catch.

He turned onto his belly then too, and somehow he was closer than before. She wasn't sure he realised it but she did. She could see the little hairs on his arms, the elongated biceps as he stretched for his glass.

This was crazy. Why was she noticing these things? Sure, she knew the power of attraction, the way two people could click, the way chemicals could align into hot sex. And the way the buzz disappeared just as quickly afterwards. Hell, she'd had her fair share of casual flings but never had her awareness hormones been on such high alert as now. She was *very* aware of Lucas Beaufort.

She stretched out on the rug, letting the last of the sun's rays warm her limbs. She looked at the tiny beach area in front of his amazing duck-egg-blue craftsman-style house. The sky was streaked with reds and oranges as the sun sank. And there was no one else but them. 'I like it here. It feels as if no one is watching.'

'I thought you liked to be watched.' Again the raised eyebrow. 'Don't you want to take some selfies and post them on the internet to let everyone know what you're up to? The unspoilt beach that will inevitably become spoiled once everyone's visited it. Pictures or it hasn't happened, right?'

'Like you don't know.'

He popped an olive into his mouth and chewed. 'I'm at work for more hours in the day than I care to think about. I don't have time to do social media but lots of people do. That's okay. I believe yours is quite popular.'

'It was. *The Princess Pages*. The blog, the website and later 'the gram'. She rolled onto her back and shuddered at the memories of the things she'd written; although they'd been heartfelt at the time, they'd also had a lot of shock factor. 'That was a long time ago. And a very—how should I describe it?—successful way of expressing my anger and frustration and teenage angst, rather than using the platform for good. Papa was horrified and with good reason. But I'm twenty-eight, Lucas. It's time to be an adult, *si*? And that means focusing on others and not myself.' She chose not to mention the real reason behind her sudden forced maturity and why she'd stopped being the Party Princess. 'I'm opening a hospital for the people of Isola Verde.'

'You're building a hospital?' Lucas looked impressed.

'Not actually building—I have people to do that for me. But yes. It's much needed. At the moment we have to go to Naples for anything more than a GP can handle. That's difficult and dangerous if it's an emergency. Our people need something on the island and I'm making it happen. It was a fight to find the right place, to raise the capital and get the backers. And to get Papa on board.'

It had been a fight to get her father even remotely interested in the beginning because he hadn't had any faith in her being able to achieve it, but she was proud at how much she'd done. 'It opens in a couple of months.'

Lucas held her gaze. A frown. Deep thinking. Then his gaze dipped to her mouth and slowly trailed down to her bikini top, where she just knew her nipples were cold and pebbled.

As he met her gaze again something heated in his eyes that was surprising, even though it mirrored the way her body was reacting to him. Admiration. *More*. Interest. *More*.

Sexual interest.

And still he kept on looking and she looked right back. The stark rawness of need that suffused her body and prickled her skin made her mouth suddenly wet. It had been a long time since she'd been so intensely physically attracted to someone and it felt like a visceral awakening.

He swallowed and she just knew he felt the connection too. 'You've changed, Giada.'

'I hope so.' She picked up her glass. 'I've put my…difficult past behind me but it's going to take a while to forget the things I did and the people I hurt—my father, mainly, as he was the one embarrassed by every scandal. What's the worst thing you ever did?'

'Inhaled, probably.' He winked and for the first time in the hours since she'd met him he actually smiled. 'I am not prepared to divulge anything else.'

She almost choked on her water. Not just at the lack of anything bad in his past but at the way his face completely changed with just the smallest of smiles. Relaxed, he was simply beautiful. His eyes lit up and his mouth… God, that mouth. What would it be like to kiss him?

It was going to be a very long three days if every time she looked at Lucas she felt all turned on and achy. 'Before this weekend is over I want to know all the dirt on you, Lucas Beaufort. Dom says the only thing you've ever committed to is being a bachelor.'

'I've had my share of relationships. I just haven't publicised them. Or had any that held my interest for long.'

He was definitely single. Interesting. That made two of them…

'Pick up any Isola Verde rag and you can read about every single sorry relationship I ever had. The stupidity of youth, right?'

The corner of his mouth tipped. 'You were young; people understand that.'

'It took me a long time to grow up.'

Lucas turned onto his side to face her, propped up on his elbow. 'Growing up is overrated. I've been doing it for longer than I care to remember.'

She imagined him as an earnest child, studying his books with that little frown over his eyes. Dom had said he'd met Lucas in a locker room at the hospital all screwed up in anger over some family argument. Her brother had talked him down and they'd been firm friends ever since, so he must be a good man. A sexy as hell man. But he was far too serious.

She wanted to poke him or tickle him with a blade of grass to see if he'd laugh, but thought better of it. Hell, with any other guy she fancied she'd have just gone and done it. But with Lucas she wasn't sure. She couldn't read him, and that made him even more alluring. Instead of tickling him, she looked right into those eyes that were the same colour as her beloved Isola Verde hills. 'So let's pretend we're kids again this weekend. Let's play a little.'

For the briefest of moments he looked like a child who'd been offered ice cream…and had then remembered he was allergic to dairy products. His gaze clashed with hers and she could tell he knew exactly what she was suggesting. 'No, Giada.'

'That's it? No?'

'No.' He was determined, she could see. And yet…wavering. The way he looked at her mouth made her ache to kiss him. It wouldn't take much, just breaching the gap between them. Not far at all…

'What would you do if you could do anything at all?' she asked him.

He said nothing, just reached for a stray lock of her hair and let it run through his fingers. He contemplated her for a very long time. So long she'd almost forgotten what she'd asked him. Although the closeness, the heating of her skin and his scent mingling with the fresh cool air made her playful proposal very front and centre. It was there. They could grab it.

And still they just stared at each other until she could finally read what was going through his mind just by the way his eyes reacted.

Could they?

Should they?

Somehow they'd moved towards each other until they were touching. She felt the beat of his heart against her chest. The warm, soft breeze of his breath on her shoulder. His lips parted.

He was so close. 'Right now, Gigi, I want to kiss you.'

Oh, wow. Her tummy fluttered. Her breasts ached. She put her hand to his chest, felt the soft skin under her fingertips, the hard muscle under that. Heard his sharp intake of breath at her touch. He ran his thumb over her mouth and she heard a whimper come from her throat.

Then he drew back.

What? No one ever refused her. Not like this.

'Do it,' she urged. Almost willing to beg.

'No way.'

This was one of those once-in-a-lifetime chances. Feeding a raw need that had sprung up from…from what? Serendipity? Magic? An electric charge between them so damned bright it could light up the whole of Seattle. 'Do it, Lucas.'

There was so much heat in his dark gaze. 'No. One, you're the Princess of Isola Verde and if we do anything and it gets out, we'll both be toast.

Two, I am ten years older than you. And, three, you're my best friend's sister.'

'Ah, that famous bro code again. But does Dom actually need to know? Hell, he practically forced me on you this weekend.'

'No, he didn't. He had a clash in his timetable and he asked me to help. To *help*, Gigi. That's a trust thing, okay? He would kill me if you and I stepped over a line.'

'Like this?' She wound her leg between his and aligned her body along his. God, he felt good. 'How would he ever know? Would you tell him?'

His eyes darkened. 'Never.'

'And neither would I.' She leaned closer, his lips a millimetre away.

'What's the punishment for kissing the King's daughter? Beheading?' He finally laughed, and it was the best sound she'd ever heard. Deep and yet melodic. Freeing.

She wanted to hear it again, wanted to make him smile, and she knew the best way to do that. Lost in him, she cupped his jaw. She could not stop this.

She pressed her mouth to his. The electricity was off the scale. Shocking. Intense. Amazing. Dangerous.

'It's got to be worth losing your head over, right? Just once. Or…maybe twice? Just for the weekend. No one needs to know. And phooey to the age gap. Who cares?' In truth, seducing an older, in-control man was a lot sexier than a younger hook-up. 'We could just…play. *Dio*, I need that and you do too. You're always so serious. Let's have some fun.' She saw the moment he made his decision. His eyes misted with the same need she felt.

'Gigi.' The way he said her name made heat pool deep in her belly. Then his mouth was on hers and he was laying her down on his private beach, her limbs warmed from the sun and liquid from desire.

His kiss was as demanding and desperate as she felt. A kiss that stoked the deepest parts of her, making her press against him, feeling the hard ridge between them. Making her want more. All of him. Here. Now. Pure lust. Raw need.

It was liberating to just be herself, Gigi Baresi, just a normal girl with a red-hot guy, making out on a beach.

Her idea of heaven…

CHAPTER ONE

November

IF EVER THERE was a time to play the royal card, it was now...

But the need to keep everything under the radar about the accident: her father, the reason they were in the United States en route to Seattle General Hospital and about...she pressed her hand to her belly and closed her eyes...*everything* was paramount. Secrecy was key.

Which made the screeching sirens, the ambulances and code red alert all the more ironic. Gigi didn't think her heart had stopped racing since the moment their car had skidded out of control on the ice. The concrete barrier looming up too fast. The impact. Her screams. Her dad's pained moans. Then his silence.

Her papa.

No matter how difficult things had been between them or how much she'd wanted to escape her life, she had never wanted something like this to happen.

'Another patient came in just before me. My father. He was in the car accident. Roberto Baresi?' she asked the nurse who was examining the painful welt across Gigi's chest. 'Can you find out what's happening with him? Is he okay? He was bleeding a lot and he…he was unconscious.'

The nurse—'Kat' it said on her name badge—shook her head. 'I'm sorry, I don't know, but he's in good hands. I'll find out more as soon as I can, and I promise I'll let you know. Right now I need to focus on your injuries. Are you sure you have no tightness in your chest? There's a nasty bruise blooming there. No abdominal pain?'

Gigi took a deep breath and checked the way she felt. 'No chest tightness.'

Just blind panic. Her thoughts jumped from one thing to the next. And everything looked bad.

Was now a good time to mention she was pregnant? Probably. But she had to wait. She didn't want everyone knowing, least of all her brother— the head of this freaking emergency department! And word would definitely get to him. He would read her notes. He'd find out and who knew what would happen then. Her whole life would blow up. The whole nation of Isola Verde would catch fire with gossip and innuendo. *Again.*

And it wasn't fair to Lucas that everyone knew before he did.

'Good. You had a lucky call there. That seatbelt probably saved your life.' Kat nodded. 'You said your wrist hurt. Can I have a look at that?'

Gigi held out her arm for the nurse to prod and poke. 'Ouch. *Sì*, that hurts. But it's nothing. It's fine.'

'I don't like the look of it. I'm worried it could be broken. I'll get one of the doctors to order an X-ray for you.'

'An X-ray? Oh, no. No way.' She couldn't let that happen. She knew about the danger of X-rays and foetuses. *Baby. It's a baby. My baby.*

Our baby, she checked herself. What was he going to say when she told him? She'd been avoiding it for so long. Thirteen long weeks, to be precise. Gigi pulled herself together; she'd given the nurse such an over-the-top reaction to a sensible suggestion it would only raise more questions. 'I mean… I'm sorry, but is it really necessary just for a bit of swelling? I don't want to take up any more of your time and resources.'

Kat nodded. 'It's the only way we can know for sure if it's broken.'

This was a nightmare. If she point blank refused the X-ray it'd be suspicious. Gigi tugged her hand from the nurse's gentle grip. 'I'm sorry to be a pain, but if anyone's going to examine me it has to be Dr Lucas Beaufort. Is he around?'

The nurse frowned. 'He's with another patient.'

'I need to speak to him. Can you please tell him that Giada is here?' She managed to control the wobble in her voice, but not the wobble in her lip. Hot damn. She could not cry here. 'Now, please.'

Before I self-combust.

What about the baby? She wanted to yell. She wanted to demand a scan. To scream at everyone about the unfairness of all this. She wanted to rewind the clock until before they'd got into the car, before they'd arrived in the country. Before she'd spent the weekend with Lucas.

Instead of screaming, she cloaked herself in full, royal, Isola Verdian fortitude. *Remember who you are. You're Princess Giada Francesca Vittoria Baresi.* He might have been lying on a hospital gurney, but her father's words would stay with her for ever.

'Nurse Kat, I'd appreciate it if you could find Lucas as a matter of urgency.'

'Of course.' The nurse nodded and stood back. If she was taken aback by Gigi's response then she hid it well under a mask of professionalism.

Which made Gigi feel worse. Hell, she'd spent enough time getting Isola Verde's new hospital ready to know the dedication and hard work the medics put into their jobs. 'I'm sorry, I didn't mean to snap at you. I just need to speak to him.'

The adrenalin was wearing off now and Gigi was starting to tremble. She felt tears prick at the backs of her eyes. Scenes from the accident flashed across her mind. Snapshots of fear. Pain. The sound of metal crunching. The bang. Her father being worked on, their bodyguard covered in blood and—

Oddio, how was he? How had this happened?

Her brother had only managed fleeting eye contact with her before she'd sent him to see their papa and the others who'd been in the car and so far there'd been no news about any of them.

So she was stuck here, alone. And cold. She couldn't risk anyone finding out that Domenico was her brother and the heir to the throne…a throne he may well have to step into immediately if their father didn't pull through. A throne he didn't want. On an island he didn't even call home any more.

Her father might die. She had a baby inside her and she didn't know if it was okay. She didn't know if anything was going to be okay. Everything was going to change and she wasn't ready. Suddenly she felt very frightened and very alone and her body hurt from the impact.

She gripped Kat's arm with her good hand. There was nothing else to do but find someone to help her, and the only someone she could think of was the father of her baby. Even though he had no idea what was about to hit him. 'Please. Please, find Lucas.'

'Blood pressure dropping. Systolic seventy-five. We need to get him to Theatre *now* and fix that haemorrhaging.' Lucas looked down at the old man's pale face. He was holding on, but with a serious open leg fracture and possible head injury Lucas didn't know for how long. He nodded at Emilia, the talented orthopaedic surgeon about to take care of the nasty leg break and hopefully stem the blood loss. 'Ready?'

She nodded. 'I'll take it from here. Thanks, Lucas.'

'Good luck, not that you'll need it.' He removed his hands from his patient's head and let the anaesthesiologist take over care of his airway, then watched the flurry of activity from the staff as they hurriedly raced their patient towards Theatre, managing his lifesaving adjunct fluid therapy and balancing beeping monitors on the gurney. Then he snapped off his gloves and tapped out a history on the patient file on the computer.

Once done, he left Resus and rounded the corner, almost bumping into one of the ER nurses,

Kat. She smiled. 'Oh, Lucas. Glad I've found you. There's a patient here demanding to see you and only you.'

'Oh?'

'Yes. MVA. Nasty bruising from the seatbelt and a swollen, painful wrist. Refusing any care at all, unless she's seen by you.' Kat gave him a quizzical look. 'Weird, right?'

'Why me?'

'A secret admirer?' Kat winked.

'Somehow, I don't think so.' He laughed at such a preposterous thought. He didn't need this right now. 'Has she been in before?'

'No. First time. At least, there's no other notes on the system for her. She came in with the patient that's just gone to Theatre. Roberto Baresi. She's his daughter, I think. Giada Baresi, I think she said.'

The floor under Lucas's feet felt as if it was shifting. 'Giada's here? Giada was in the car? In the MVA?' How had he missed that?

Because he'd been so focused on saving that man's life he'd paid no attention either to his name or to what else was happening in the department. Hell. His gut tightened like a vice. 'Where is she? Is she hurt?'

'Room nine. Her wrist's…'

He didn't stop to hear the rest of Kat's handover. Giada was here and she was hurting, everything else was immaterial.

As he dashed down the corridor his mind filled in the blanks. If the patient going into Theatre was Giada and Dom's father he was also…the King of Isola Verde. Yet no one had mentioned it—not even Dom, who had overseen his own father's initial care. Which surely meant that no one else knew and that must be for a reason…so he would keep it that way for his friend's sake.

Lucas's heart rate doubled. Poor Dom, to be faced with the only two members of his family injured and in his hospital. Every medic's nightmare. Lucas determined that after seeing Giada he'd seek out his friend and see how he was holding up. Be there for him. For them all. The way Dom had been there for Lucas over the years, as if he were a brother.

But, then, trouble often stemmed from families too. It was always about families. The good, the bad and the estranged.

Giada.

'Lucas?' She looked up as he threw open the door to her room. Her face was pale, her dark brown eyes huge as she sat on a plastic chair next to the examination couch, looking vulnerable and strained. Completely opposite from the way she'd looked that weekend months ago—vibrant, sexy, full of fun.

'Lucas.' She stood up and he could see the angry welt slashed across her skin, from her collar bone to the edge of her pale blue sweater.

'Gigi. My God.' He didn't know a heart could feel as if it had completely stopped and yet race at double speed at the same time. Didn't know he'd feel like this when he saw her again, awash with emotions he couldn't put a name to.

And he certainly didn't know what the right thing to do was. They'd put royal protocol aside three months ago, but things were very different now. He went to her but waited for her to make a move. This was a long way from sex on the beach. A million miles from two people enjoying each other just for one weekend.

Ciao, Captain Sensible. You dark horse, you. Thanks for taking care of all my...needs!

That smile. The wink. She'd drawn out a different side of him that weekend, but the fun had stopped the minute he'd delivered her to the private airfield and ever since he'd been...

This was not the time for that. 'Gigi, the nurse said you're hurt.'

Nodding, she stood, before swaying a little and stepping into his arms, clinging to him. '*Oddio.* Lucas, I can't stop shaking. It was... Is he going to be okay? Is Papa going to die? And what about his bodyguard? He was injured too.'

'It's okay, Gigi. I'm here.' He stroked her hair,

battling the whoosh of emotions besieging him as her scent wound round him, as muscle memory made his hands fit round her waist exactly… there. As his body found space for her.

She had a way of hugging that was full contact. At least, a way of hugging *him* that felt as if she was giving everything to it. And he held her close, waiting for the ragged breathing to subside, the same way he'd held her on the beach, in his kitchen, in his bed and watched her come down from the throes of ecstasy.

But this was very different.

They stood like that for a minute, maybe more. Touch was their vocabulary and comfort.

Her touch had driven him crazy with desire only months ago and he hadn't realised he'd been craving it ever since. And yet they'd both agreed it would be a single weekend in a lifetime. No more. There just couldn't be more.

Now she was here and he didn't know what to do to make her feel better.

He mentally shook himself. He was a representative of Seattle General Hospital, a senior doctor and medical professional. He could compartmentalise three days from the rest of his life. He had to be the utmost professional now, especially with her brother breathing down his neck and her father in surgery. Added to the fact she was European royalty with a destiny very different from his.

Eventually she pulled away and breathed out deeply, tugging on a mask of coping. 'Okay. Thank you. I think I was starting to fall apart. I'm okay now.'

'You don't have to pretend, Gigi. You're allowed to fall apart at times like this.' He put a little distance between them and adopted his usual professional tone. 'Your papa is in Theatre. He's had a nasty leg injury and he was unconscious when the paramedics brought him in so we're a little worried about a brain injury—especially with the complications of his tumour.'

'You know about that?' Her eyes widened.

'A few of the more senior staff are aware that a VIP is scheduled for neurosurgery on a tumour in about three weeks' time. Dom confided to me that it was your father.'

'Of course he did.' Her hands worried at the hem of her sweater that was frayed and blood spattered. 'This is so bad.'

'As soon as we've stabilised him we'll take him for a brain scan. We won't know anything for a little while, but he's in good hands. Emilia's the best orthopaedic surgeon we have.'

She pressed her lips together as blood drained from her face. He took her hands and led her back to the chair. 'Sit down. You're in shock. That seatbelt trauma looks painful. Do you need something to help with the pain?'

'No!' She shook her head sharply. 'No drugs. I'll be fine.'

'Okay, okay.' She was clearly traumatised. He tried to make his tone gentler. 'Can I have a look at that wrist now?'

She nodded again, her eyes brimming with unshed tears as she held out the swollen and bruised arm to him. 'Kat said it might need an X-ray.'

'I'd say so.' He turned her hand over to assess the damage, hating himself for hurting her even though it was necessary to ascertain the diagnosis. 'The problem with wrists is that you can't always get a good view of the injury, so even if we don't see anything today, it may be necessary to repeat an X-ray further down the track, just to be sure.'

'Can we be sure *without* an X-ray?'

'Not really. It will mean you'd have to come back here if you're still in town. Or you could arrange to have a repeat X-ray at your new hospital in Isola Verde.' She'd been so excited about her new venture, to the point that he'd felt that excitement too.

She looked up at him through curls that had fallen over her face. 'I can't have an X-ray, Lucas.'

'It won't take much time. We'll have you all

strapped up before your father gets out of surgery. You can go to him then.'

'That's not what I mean. Lucas...' She ran the back of her good hand across her forehead and blew out a slow breath. 'Lucas, I...'

'What?'

She blinked. 'I wasn't supposed to be coming with Papa for this trip. It was organised very last minute because he wanted to see Domenico about...well, about what might happen if he didn't make it out of surgery—'

'I'm sure he'll be fine. I understand his neurosurgeon for the tumour surgery is already on his way from Vancouver to discuss your father's case with the surgeons here.'

'... If he's incapable of ruling Isola Verde and the implications that has for Domenico,' she continued.

'God. Yes. Of course. Dom would become King and have to leave here and...' Dom loved his job. Loved Seattle. He hadn't been home to Isola Verde for years. Although he hadn't actually said it out loud, Lucas had a feeling that Dom was a very reluctant heir to the throne. 'They need to talk.'

'Yes, very much. Now we don't know if they ever will. Papa is frail...was frail even before this accident, and he's determined to bring Domenico back home as soon as possible. He needs his son with him to pass over a lot of royal duties.' Gigi sighed. 'But that wasn't why I came. I can't be the intermediary between the King and the heir.' She sighed again, her face creasing with concern. 'I needed to see you. To talk to you, Lucas.'

She needed to talk to him and she sure as hell wasn't professing her undying love for him. In fact, she looked apprehensive, scared even.

Lucas prided himself on being logical. On working out difficult conundrums, hard-to-solve cases.

She didn't want an X-ray. Why not? What was it about X-rays?

She didn't want drugs.

He looked at her beautiful pale face, scanned down to her full breasts. Her belly that looked just as flat as when he'd been with her. But…

But…

She put her hand over his. 'This isn't how I planned to do this, Lucas. But you have to know—'

She didn't need to tell him; he'd worked it out. 'You're pregnant.'

She nodded and looked so distraught about the whole damned situation that he had to look away.

Unable to bear the raw intimacy of her touch and the memories that brought, he pulled his hand out from under hers. Then he stepped away too,

the ramifications hitting him from every angle,
jabbing at him like knives.

A baby? His baby? With the Princess of Isola
Verde?

What the hell had they done?

CHAPTER TWO

GIADA'S HEART FRACTURED as she watched Lucas take a step back. Two steps.

In fact, if the door hadn't been closed she imagined he'd have kept on retreating right out of the hospital, across the city, through Olympic National Park, over the water and as far away as Japan.

This was not the way she'd imagined telling him. So raw and brutal.

This was also not the reaction she'd wanted. Expected, yes. Wanted? Not so much. A smile, perhaps. A claim on their child. A hug. A promise that everything would be okay.

But, then, she'd known Lucas had been serious when he'd talked about not breaking the best friend code. Plus…okay, so she was a princess. Which made everything a million times more complicated. Pregnant and single. That would certainly attract more headlines. Although, given her reputation, it probably wouldn't surprise her people. But her father would be singularly un-impressed.

Again.

She hid her head in her hands and sighed deeply.

'I didn't intend this to happen, Lucas. I'm…' She was not going to be sad about the baby. 'Actually, I'm not sorry. Sure, it's a surprise and it took a bit of getting used to, not to mention the morning sickness. But I'm having a baby and that should be cause for celebration.' And she *was* happy. Now she'd got over the shock.

When she looked up he was still standing there, rigid, looking at her as if trying to work out a very difficult and shocking puzzle. 'Lucas. Please. Say something.'

He blinked and shook his head. 'You'll need a scan. Contracting seatbelts can cause damage to the abdomen and the uterus. I'll get the radiographer to bring the portable machine in here.'

So they were going the emotionless route. Right. 'Thank you. But I'd know, surely? If something was wrong. There'd be bleeding or pain and I don't have either.'

'We need to check.'

'Yes. Yes, please.' She'd thought he'd leave then to speak to the radiographer, but he made a quick call and stayed in the room. Silent.

After a few moments and just to say something

to break the hideous impasse, she said, 'You're going to stay for the scan?'

'Of course. I might be in shock but I'm not a monster, Giada.' Not Gigi. Back to Giada. 'You must be, what, twelve, thirteen weeks? Why didn't you tell me before?'

'I wanted to be sure. Risk of miscarriage is higher before twelve weeks so I figured that if I lost the baby I wouldn't need to tell you anything. And then we wouldn't have this awkward scenario going on. But this little one...' she skimmed a hand across her abdomen '...is here to stay. As soon as everything was confirmed I arranged to come with Papa.'

He captured her gaze with dark, untrusting eyes. 'You didn't know I was going to be here.'

'You're always at work, Lucas. That's what you told me. If you hadn't been here I would have called, but I wanted to tell you face to face.'

The door swung open and an older woman walked in pushing a large trolley with a machine on it. 'Ultrasound machine as requested, Dr Beaufort. You want me to do it?'

Lucas frowned. 'Yes.'

'Oh?' So much for the privacy she'd been hoping for. 'I thought you'd do it.'

'Sure, for a heartbeat, but not the full antenatal scan you need to have, given the circumstances.' One minute he'd been holding her, the next he was back-pedalling as fast and as far as his good manners would allow. Oh, Lucas Beaufort was good at cutting off his emotions.

Very interesting, and a smack in the face to her. That weekend had been the only time she'd felt seen for who she was as a person and not as the tabloid Princess. He'd wanted to explore her and not judge her. But now? Now she wasn't sure how the man she'd spent the weekend with could be the same cold one standing here.

Sure, he was serious by nature, and he'd been bogged down with the bro code and her being a princess and everything, but once he'd got over that he'd been very hot indeed.

She looked at him now, at his darkened eyes and clenched jaw that told her he was struggling to stay in control. At his dark blond hair, remembering the way it had felt as she'd thrust her fingers into it in the throes of ecstasy. She shivered, surprised at the hot, sharp, tang of lust that rippled through her even now. Even when he was angry and confused and aloof.

He nodded towards the machine. 'Obstetric scanning is a highly skilled process and, while I know enough to get by, I don't want to miss anything.'

Or he didn't want to touch her.

Stung by his reaction, Gigi climbed onto the examination couch and lifted her now ruined cashmere sweater to bare her belly, then wriggled her trousers down to her hips.

Lucas looked away.

She tried to read him but he'd simply closed off. Was he staying for the scan because he thought he should? Or because he wanted to? For her? For the baby?

But these weren't the kinds of questions she could ask with an audience, especially in the hospital where Lucas and her brother worked.

'Bit of jelly. Here we go.' The sonographer smiled and squirted gel onto Gigi's belly, which had grown just a tiny bit over the last few weeks. She was almost breathless at the pride she had in the teeniest bit of a bump. 'What was the date of your last period, Giada?'

She didn't need to look it up. 'Tenth of August.'

She saw Lucas do the maths and nod.

'Which makes you…?' The sonographer took a cardboard wheel out and turned it, but before she could check Gigi jumped in. 'Thirteen weeks.'

She'd counted every single day from the first day her period was late, wishing it would happen, praying for her usual cramping, hoping the painful breasts were PMT symptoms, trying to ignore the queasiness and the throwing up. Slowly getting used to the idea that she was very definitely pregnant and wondering how, seeing as they'd used condoms. But maybe…had they… every time…? Or had one failed?

Either way, she was having a baby. His baby.

She tried to look at Lucas to make eye contact to say, *See, it is yours*, in case he'd been in any doubt, but he was focused on the ultrasound screen. She knew without doubt because she hadn't slept with anyone else for a very long time. Ever since the last ill-advised lover had tried to blackmail her. Just another *cretino* trying to gain celebrity from her royal status. Way to grow up pretty fast.

'And your last scan was…?'

'Last week.' There'd been no way she was going to go to her newly opened hospital and advertise her pregnancy to everyone there, so she'd sneaked out to a private clinic and made them promise not to tell a living soul her news. 'They said they couldn't accurately tell the gender, but I didn't want to know. Other than that, all was fine.'

More than fine. She'd seen their baby properly for the first time and hadn't been able to tell a single person about it. Sure, she had friends, but she'd learnt a long time ago that entrusting people with a princess's deeply personal information could backfire. Spectacularly.

Lucas's back was taut, his whole body coiled tight as he growled, 'Can we just get on with it?'

'Sorry, Dr Beaufort. I know you're busy.' The

sonographer nodded as if used to Lucas's sharp manner.

Well, Gigi wasn't. 'Please, take your time. It's better to be thorough, right? Make sure everything is okay.'

Lucas looked at his feet. 'Absolutely. Yes. Take your time.'

The room was filled the with fast *whoosh-um whoosh-um-whoosh-um* of a heartbeat. Gigi turned to look at the screen and saw the grey blurry shapes the sonographer was pointing out. The four chambers of the heart. Four long limbs…like his or her father. A cute nub nose. Perfect.

She hadn't realised she'd been holding her breath, but now she exhaled on a long sigh and, just like during her last scan, her own heart made more space for this child, and her chest filled with warmth and light. Whatever Lucas thought about it, whatever he decided to do was his choice, but she would love this baby with everything she had.

'Is it okay?' he asked, his voice catching a little.

She turned her head to watch as he peered at the screen. The stiffness of his limbs was gone. There was a softening in his eyes that made her heart squeeze. He wasn't cold-hearted, he was just in shock.

'Everything's fine.' The sonographer smiled. 'You have a little wriggler here.'

'I do—? I mean, she does?' Lucas blinked. Coughed. 'That's good news. Right. Thank you.'

'I can capture a photograph for you,' the sonographer told Gigi. 'A video too, if you like.'

'That would be lovely, thank you.' She'd brought a copy of the last scan with her to show Lucas, to give to him if he wanted it. Now he could have two. 'If you email it to me, I can send it on to the father,' she said with an eye on Lucas.

He nodded, his face unreadable; if he wanted the scan he didn't indicate it in any way. But he asked in an unemotional tone as the sonographer set the printer in motion, 'Could I borrow the ultrasound machine for a few minutes? Giada has a painful, swollen arm and, given the circumstances, I'd prefer to do an ultrasound rather than an X-ray.' Lucas turned to Gigi. 'The development of the baby's central nervous system happens between ten and seventeen weeks, so being exposed to an X-ray during that time period is ill-advised. An ultrasound is not as accurate a diagnostic tool, but it can give us a good indication of whether there is a fracture. That I am more than happy to do by myself.'

Gigi nodded, trying to translate not just his words but his manner. Having been reassured that all was well with the baby, he'd snapped back from father to medic. 'Lover' had completely disappeared at the mention of pregnancy.

'Great,' the sonographer said. 'I'm due a break now anyway, so I'll collect the machine in fifteen minutes.'

Gigi's heart clenched. Because, sure, there was a lot they needed to say to each other but the thought of being alone again with a very shocked Lucas filled her with dread.

This wasn't going well.

Lucas concentrated on keeping his hand steady as he ran the probe over Gigi's right wrist. Keeping it steady, because he was damned sure his whole body was about to shake and he didn't know how he was going to stop it.

A baby. *Damn.* It was the last thing he'd ever wanted. And with a woman he'd spent only three days with, a woman who had a future all mapped out that was very different from what he'd been working towards his whole life. Family wasn't something he did well. And he hadn't ever wanted to get invested in something that could be so quickly erased from his life, the way he had been from his parents' and siblings' lives.

And with Gigi being settled in Isola Verde and his life here in Seattle, it was very likely that he would be erased. What if she fell in love and married someone else? Would he still be seen as the father then? Would he have access rights to a royal child? How would something long distance work out? Hours spent on aircraft for both him and the little one.

Perhaps marriage was the only way of tethering himself to his child.

But…marriage? To the Princess of Isola Verde? As if that would be allowed to happen.

He was getting way ahead of himself.

Trouble was, he worked hard to keep his distance from any kind of family trap but the minute he'd seen the baby on the screen he'd claimed it in his heart. It was a living thing, a part of him. He felt blindsided by panic, and hugely protective.

As for Gigi…there was so much they needed to talk about that he didn't know where to start. Luckily, emotionless, reliable scientific logic was his go-to, so he started with that.

'I can't see any fractures. There's a lot of tissue oedema…that is, swelling. I recommend rest, elevation and strapping. A sling will help remind you not to use it and give support that will help the pain. If you need pain relief then acetaminophen will be fine, under the—'

'The circumstances, right?' she snapped. 'The circumstances being that I'm carrying your child and you're not happy about it.'

Happy? It was the worst thing that could possibly happen…a Baresi baby. Their baby.

He couldn't put how he was feeling into words. 'I've only just found out, Giada. Give me a moment to adjust. We need to sit down and talk about it rationally, once you're feeling up to it. But not right now, okay? You have enough to deal with.'

'I know.' She stared down at her bruised and misshapen hand, her eyes hollowed out, and sighed sadly. 'A very sick father, a pregnancy and a damaged dominant hand. Could it get any worse?'

Try suddenly finding out you're a father.

She needed support but he wasn't sure he was the person to offer it. 'Do you know anyone in Seattle?'

'Other than Dom and you? No.'

'Where are you staying?'

'At… Wait, I can't remember.' Frowning, she plucked her phone from her bag and scrolled through. 'The Four Seasons.'

'On your own?'

'Now, yes, I suppose so. I don't know.' Her eyes wandered around the room as if the answers were here somewhere. 'Obviously Papa is here. We had rooms booked at the Four Seasons, but I don't know what to do now. The car's totalled so I'll have to get a taxi to the hotel, I suppose. I don't know.' She ran the back of her hand across her forehead and her shoulders collapsed forward. 'I don't know what to do.'

He tried not to feel anything as he looked at her

because feelings only hampered good sense but it was no use—every time his eyes met hers he was back in bed, tumbling with her in the sheets. 'You look exhausted.'

Blinking fast, she straightened and seemed to snap herself back together. 'I'm fine.'

This was the Giada who'd arrived at his house. The one who'd pretended not to be stung by his initial refusal to play with her. The one who'd become used to dealing with her problems on her own and hated being seen as weak for wanting basic human connection.

He couldn't imagine how she was feeling given the stress she was under and the pain from the car crash. He wasn't being fair by being so standoffish so he softened his tone. 'Okay. You've been travelling for hours. The flight took how long?'

'Twelve hours.'

'Then the stress and adrenalin…none of that is good for the baby. You need to rest.'

At the mention of their child she looked directly at him. 'I understand that stress isn't good for our baby, Lucas, but unfortunately I'm dealing with a lot right now. I need to know what's happening with Papa. I won't leave here until I know he's going to be okay. And someone has to run my country, work out how much, if anything, to say to the nation. I'm going to have to try to talk Dom into going back to Isola Verde.

He won't want to. But that's why we came here in the first place. To talk to him about taking over some of Papa's duties. I'm repeating myself, I think. I have such a bad headache.'

'Okay.' She was still in shock and panicked. The adrenalin would be whirring through her system, sending her thoughts scattering. He had to take control. He knelt in front of her. 'Let's make a plan. We'll deal with your wrist then I'll find out about your father, and I'll take you to your hotel.'

She sat back and sighed. 'Thank you.'

'And we'll stop off and get you something to eat. You need food.' He was interrupted by his phone's shrill tone. 'It's Dom.'

Her eyes grew wide and panicked. 'Don't tell him about the baby. Please. Please don't say anything. We need to work things out, you and me, before we say anything to anyone.'

Lucas didn't know how they were even going to begin that conversation. 'Yes, but after you've had a rest.'

She touched the back of his hand as he went to answer the call. 'Please don't say—'

'Giada, stop. Of course I won't say anything. I've got to work all this out in my head before I say or do anything else.' He pressed the call answer button. 'Hey, bro. You okay?'

'Holding up. Are you with Gigi? Kat said she was asking for you.'

'Yes, Giada's here.' He stood up and walked to the window, more for space from Giada than privacy. The room was so small she'd hear everything anyway. 'Just finished examining her wrist.'

'Is there a break?'

'No.' If…no, *when…* Dom heard about the pregnancy there would be a million questions and no doubt the inevitable betrayal accusation slung at him. Lucas didn't want to think about what this baby might do to his friendship with Dom, but for now he was going to be the best mate he could be. 'I'm organising compression and support. She's going to need to rest it for a few days.'

'That's not going to go down well with my dynamo sister. Is there anything else? Is she okay?'

She's pregnant. So, no, things weren't okay, at least not in Lucas's world.

But Gigi was clearly happy about it, judging by the look of relief on her face the second they'd heard the heartbeat.

'She's holding up, a bit shocked but getting there.' He turned and met her eyes and couldn't read what was going through her head. She held his gaze and he remembered how she'd tried every which way to make him laugh.

Come on, Captain Sensible. Stop being so serious.

She'd tickled and poked him, made lame jokes, had had him playing tourist in his own city, and he had laughed, so much, for three delicious days, feeling the lightest he'd felt in years. But now the tables were turned and the only thing he wanted to see from her was a smile instead of the hollowed-out eyes and the bruises.

One weekend was all they'd wanted and expected from each other. Without question she'd accepted who he was and what he'd made of his life. In fact, she'd respected him, and had made him proud of what he'd achieved. She hadn't made any demands on him, apart from lots of damned good sex. That was all, in reality. Nothing to hang a relationship on.

The baby changed everything.

He didn't want to be a father. Didn't want his messed-up genes passed on to anyone.

Tough luck. It was in her troubled gaze now, as if she could read his thoughts. *We're in this together, so deal with it.*

Swallowing hard, he looked away. 'She's worried about your father and his bodyguard.'

'Tell her Logan only had some cuts and bruises and is being cleaned up. Look, my pager is blaring, I've got go. I've a million other phone calls to make while Papa is in Theatre. Tell Gigi I love her, will you? That I'll call the palace and let them know about the accident but to keep everything under wraps until we know what's going to happen next. There's royal protocol coming in to play, you see.'

'I understand.' He didn't really. Couldn't imagine the weight on his friend's shoulders right now. He imagined that by 'protocol' Dom meant a succession plan could be initiated at any moment. 'If there's anything you need me to do, Dom, just ask.'

'You know confidentiality is key here, I trust you on that. No one can know about the accident until we are sure about Papa's prognosis.' Dom breathed out heavily. 'It's enough to know Giada's in safe hands and it's one less thing for me to worry about—right now, anyway. Tell her I'll talk to her as soon as I get a chance.'

Guilt shimmied down Lucas's spine. Safe hands? Once upon a time maybe. Before that August weekend when his hands had been itching to touch Giada's body. 'Sure thing.'

'Thanks, Lucas. I can breathe a bit easier knowing I can rely on you. It's good she has someone she knows with her. Stay with her, if you can. Please. She needs a friend.'

Lucas grimaced internally—that was exactly how he'd got into this mess in the first place. But this was most certainly not the time to go there.

'Of course. No problem.' The trippy ultrasound heartbeat that had somehow connected with his own heart pushed, squeezed and wriggled its way uninvited into his chest.

You've got a little wriggler there.

He sure had. He swallowed. He pushed those thoughts away—well, banked them until later—because he wasn't ever going to stop thinking about his child.

That suddenly made him wonder why it had been so easy for his family to cut off contact with him, save for the paltry annual Christmas email that was probably the same one they sent to their insurance broker. What was it about him that had made them decide he wasn't good enough to stay in touch? To call once in a while?

Families. He just didn't understand them. 'Dom, listen, I hope your father's okay.'

'So do I. More than you could imagine.' There was a beeping in the background. 'Damn pager. Got to go. Sorry.'

God, it was awful enough to have your father in surgery not knowing if he was going to pull through, but also, Lucas guessed, Dom was praying for his father's recovery because he was torn between his life here and succeeding to the throne in Isola Verde. He just needed time to get his head around the fact he was going to be King.

Lucas knew all about family expectations and

how not abiding by them caused huge family rifts, but this was so much more than anything he'd had to go through. The freaking King of a Mediterranean nation?

He flicked his phone away and glanced up at Giada. *Gigi.* His heart tightened to see her looking so pale. It seemed that protectiveness he felt for his baby didn't dim when he looked at its mother. Which was beyond crazy. He didn't know what the future had in store but right now he would do anything to make sure nothing bad happened to either of them.

Somehow his involvement in this family had become so much more complicated than just being friends and he wasn't sure how he felt about any of it.

He put his phone away and turned to her. 'Right. Dom says your father's still in Theatre and there's no word on how it's going, but the minute he hears anything he'll let you know. Info on the others involved in the MVA is that some-one called Logan—'

Her eyes grew wider. 'Yes? His bodyguard.'

'Has just minor cuts and bruises and is being cleaned up and—'

'Actually, you should probably know that Logan isn't just a bodyguard, he's a trained army medic and he's taking up a post here next week.

Or, at least, he's supposed to be, if he's not too badly injured.'

'Logan... Dr Logan Connors?' Lucas had been briefed about the new doctor's imminent arrival but hadn't realised the guy stemming the blood flow on the King's leg wound when they'd arrived was the same Dr Connors. That explained how he'd dealt with it all so expertly. 'Dr Logan Connors is a bodyguard to the Isola Verde royal family?'

She nodded. 'A good one too and we're sad to see him go, but he has a little boy and he wants him to go to school here. Logan's family is from Seattle and he wanted to bring his son and his parents home. Caring for a child on your own is hard.'

Gigi pierced him with a sharp look, as if poking him with the future she was facing.

He chose to ignore it. They needed to talk it all through when they were calmer. And definitely not here where people could barge in and hear. But she got in first, worry biting at her features. 'Is...is Dom okay?'

'He's busy. He's got to finish his shift and, knowing him, will probably stay here far beyond that.'

She shook her pretty head, her dark hair tumbling around her shoulders. 'He works too hard.'

'He's the Head of ER, it comes with the territory. In the meantime we need to get you out of here. Hospitals are no place for people who are generally well.'

A royal eyebrow rose. 'I spend a lot of time at my hospital. It hasn't affected me.'

'Yet. There are always bugs whizzing around. I'd prefer it if we can keep you as bug free as possible for the rest of your...' He glanced at her belly. Yes. It was sinking in. 'Pregnancy.'

'Okay. But I was thinking maybe it's not such a good idea for me to go to the hotel. I don't want anything leaking out about the accident just yet, or the fact we're even here in Seattle. Not until we get the say-so from Dom.' She sat forward, cradling her swollen arm. 'I'll cancel the booking for me and Papa. And... I know this is a huge imposition, Lucas, but could I stay at your place?'

Lucas closed his eyes at that thought. Have her back in his home? Her perfume on his sheets? Torture. 'I don't think that's a good idea. I can drop you off at a different ho—'

But he broke off as he watched her try to pick up her handbag, wince and then sit back in the chair, ashen with pain. How could he be so selfish? Thinking only of how awkward it would be to have her in his home when she had so much more to deal with. 'Of course you can stay with me, Giada. You're going to need some help while you rest that arm.'

'I'm fine. I can manage. I just need to remember that I can't use it.' She gave him a wobbly smile and his world tipped. The centre of his chest tightened.

'I don't want you to just manage. You need to rest; you need someone to help you. So, first, I'm going to apply some compression to help with the swelling.' He dug through the drawers and cupboards and found a bandage. 'Hold your hand out, please.'

She watched in silence as he wove the bandage between her thumb and forefinger and back over her wrist. She was so close he could smell not just her perfume but the scent that was uniquely Gigi. The one that he wasn't sure he'd entirely erased from his bed even after numerous launderings. He felt the heat of her gaze as he wound the bandage, as gently as he could but with enough firmness to provide support. Was aware of the rise and fall of her chest, fast enough to show she was still buzzing from the adrenalin. Felt the soft whisper of her breath on his neck.

The rhythmic weaving of the bandaging gave his brain space to think and it went immediately to the way this hand and these delicate fingers had played him, teased him, touched him.

And wouldn't he know it, heat wove through him, spiking a shot of desire sharp in his belly. So damned inappropriate.

He refused to look at her, knowing she'd see the desire in his eyes, and the memories. But they were of no use: he and Giada couldn't go back or look back. They certainly couldn't rekindle any of that madness that had kept them glued to each other for seventy-odd hours of sex-fuelled bliss. They had a mess to deal with and they needed to do it with level heads.

He stepped away and rummaged for a sling. 'Now I'm going to put this arm in a sling.'

'But then I won't be able to do anything.' She looked up at him.

'That's the plan. I don't want you doing anything with this hand. Elevation helps with the swelling, which in turn helps with the pain.' He opened the sling packet and tipped out the pre-shaped triangular bandage. Stepped behind her so he could drape the sling over her head and then over her arm, trying not to step too close or to breathe in her scent again. 'Fair warning, though, I'm useless with these.'

He came back round to look at the way he'd draped it. 'Okay, so it might be upside down.'

He shifted the bandage sideways. Had another look. Twisted it another ninety degrees. 'I have two medical degrees and an advanced trauma qualification. I will not be defeated by a simple sling.'

'Something you're bad at? Surely not, Lucas

Beaufort.' The corners of her mouth twitched as he stood back and inspected it again. And then he made the fatal error of looking into her eyes.

Instead of looking away, she held his gaze.

His gut tightened. How could it be that something as simple as the organs of the human visual system were so mesmerising? So beautiful and deep? Their function was to detect light and convert it into impulses the brain interpreted as images, a purely physiological act, and yet, right now, also reflective of something as abstract as emotion. One look into those dark brown irises and he could see she was in pain, probably psychologically and emotionally as well as physically. That the joking was a cover for the fact she was desperate for something…he didn't know what. Connection? Something as simple as a hug?

More?

He didn't know if he could—or should—give her more.

He straightened the sling. 'The nurses usually do it. I'm great with endotracheal tubing or complicated suturing. Fantastic with seizures, fractures and diabetic comas, but bandaging…? Not so much. But…ah, we got there in the end.' He secured the ends under her elbow with a safety pin. 'There. This will remind you not to use the arm. At all. Doctor's orders.'

She grimaced. 'How am I going to manage with this?'

'I will help you.' It appeared he had no choice. If only she didn't smell so good. Or wasn't—he swallowed at the thought of the baby growing inside her—*pregnant*.

He dug deep for a different subject. 'Now I'm going to phone for pizza.'

'I'm not sure if I'm hungry or not but you're right, I need to eat.' Finally a smile. Funny and a little sad that the only smile he could get from her was about food and not about the prospect of spending time in his home again. 'From that deli on the corner of your road? Stone fired?'

From the deli that had made the takeout pizza they'd eaten in bed after a long afternoon of lovemaking. 'The very one.'

He picked up her bag, making sure to avoid any physical contact with her. 'I can phone ahead and it'll be ready to collect as we pass by. Then we can relax and wait for updates from Dom.'

She stopped walking. 'Relax? While my father is having surgery?'

'Bad choice of words.' Seemed he was good at saying the wrong thing. Too damned good. 'But I hope you'll be comfortable there at least.'

Because he wasn't sure he would be. Not

when he knew she was within touching distance. Things had felt a lot calmer—albeit far, far duller—when she'd been in Isola Verde.

CHAPTER THREE

WELL, THIS WAS a mistake of epic proportions.

She was clearly a lot more shocked than she'd realised if she'd thought coming back here was a good idea. Giada walked into his house, took a deep breath of the rarefied air that was pure Lucas, and was immediately assailed by memories.

The corridor where they'd had sex because they just couldn't wait to get to a bed or a couch. The kitchen where he'd prepared breakfast wearing nothing but a towel. The pool…*oddio*, that lap pool where they'd skinny-dipped in the moonlight after champagne and oysters. Magical. And afterwards they'd talked into the night about books, favourite films, everything and nothing.

God, it had only been for a weekend but it had felt so right.

And now, after his reaction about the baby news, everything felt wrong. Even she felt wrong-footed and yet it was him who'd had the mother of surprises. Or rather, the *father*…

She allowed herself a smile. He'd tried to hide his interest but she'd seen the way he'd looked at that blurry image. She just didn't know what the next step was. Not for Lucas and herself or for her family. It felt as if she was juggling a lot of balls in the air and she wasn't sure she would be able to catch any of them when they fell.

'Guest room?' she asked, knowing the answer but wanting to be sure. Things were awkward enough without more complications.

He was behind her, carrying her bags. She was so aware of him. Of the hitch in his breathing when her arm had brushed against his in the car. And the responding hitch in hers. The long slender fingers that had turned the steering wheel… fingers that had given her a lot of pleasure. The way his shirt strained across taut pec muscles she knew were honed from morning laps in the pool. That his arms were strong enough to hold her up as he'd entered her, pressing her against the bedroom wall, and, yes, in that pool.

Did he remember? And did he now feel as self-conscious as she did? As if they just couldn't find the right words to clear the air and bring them full circle back to that wall. That pool.

She wondered how he'd have reacted to her if she hadn't been pregnant. Would he be making moves on her? Would she be doing that to him? Would they have gone straight back to being lovers, feeding a renewed sexual hunger they couldn't stop?

But…everything was different now.

As if he knew what she was thinking, he clarified, 'Yes. I called and had the housekeeper make it up for you. Just down the hall. On the right.'

'I remember.' *I remember everything, Captain Sensible.* 'I think I'll grab a quick shower and change out of these clothes.'

'Do you need help?' He meant with her sling, she knew, and was being polite, not teasing or flirtatious.

'I can manage. I'm going to run a bath, I think that would be a lot easier for me.' It broke her heart the way they were being so respectfully well mannered around each other when she knew him so intimately. Knew how he tasted, what he looked like naked and sleeping. How his face lit up when he smiled. How she'd felt so safe enclosed in his arms. *Oddio*, she hadn't realised just how much she'd missed him. And missed his smile. Damn, a smile from him would be a good start. But she didn't have the energy to go searching for one right now.

Exhaustion tugged at every muscle in her body so she flopped down on the deliciously comfortable bed unable to summon any strength to remove her clothes, open her suitcase or…anything.

He nodded and put her bags on the floor. 'Are you sure you'll be okay?'

'I think so.' But her eyes were already closing.

'Do not do anything with that arm, definitely no lifting. Call me if you need help. Pizza will be waiting for you when you're ready.' He closed the door as he left and she wondered just how much he didn't want her to be here.

Not that she'd be here for long. Like her brother, she had some calls to make. She forced her eyes to snap back open and, using her good hand, she took her phone out of her bag and hit the call button for the first of many conversations she needed to have.

Lucas checked the time again. Giada had been in her room for over an hour and he wasn't sure quite what to do next. The pizza had grown cold and he'd just reheated it, hoping the smell of freshly cooked dough would summon her downstairs. But no.

He knew she was tired but she needed to eat, not just for her strength but for the baby growing inside her. And there he was; already making space in his thoughts for this new life. How would it be when she wasn't in the next room but thousands of miles away? How would he deal with the thoughts then?

He'd give her five more minutes. He slid the

pizza from the pizza stone and onto a large plate on a tray.

Then he waited. Drummed his fingers on the kitchen counter. Three minutes.

Okay. Now.

He picked up the tray of food, walked to the guest room and, juggling the tray in one hand, gently tapped on the door.

No answer.

He pushed open the door and paused as he took her in, his heart stalling as lightness filled his veins. She was curled up on her side, wrapped in a fluffy white dressing-gown, fast asleep. Her hair was damp and curling in tendrils on the pillow. Her breathing came in little gasps, not snores but almost, and the sound was so cute and funny he held in a laugh. This was the Royal Princess of Isola Verde. Softly snoring in a guest room in his Seattle home.

The robe had fallen open around her breasts, baring a nipple. Creamy brown, darker than he remembered, but he knew pregnancy could change a woman's body in many ways. She was definitely fuller, rounder. He winced as his gaze slid over the raw stripe of bruising across her chest. But his eyes didn't linger there, instead trying to glimpse her belly through the tied robe.

Hot damn. What was he doing? Ogling her?

Okay. The pizza could wait. He needed to get the hell out of here.

Reluctantly dragging his eyes away from her beautiful form, he tiptoed backwards, banged into the door, clattering the plate on the tray against the glass of sparkling water. *Damn.*

'Lucas?' She sat up and rubbed her eyes.

'Sorry, didn't mean to wake you, but I thought you might be hungry.'

'Oh, the pizza? Yes. Actually, I'm starving.'

'D'you want to eat here? Or in the kitchen?'

'Here, please. I'm too tired to get off this bed. Is that okay?' She was being so polite.

'Totally fine.' He put the tray on the bed and helped her to shuffle up and recline against the pillows, making sure to elevate her sore arm. 'I hope you're ambidextrous.'

'What?' She noticed her robe had fallen open and hurriedly tugged it across her chest and tied it more tightly, but not before she caught his gaze. She knew he'd been looking. Her eyes heated, just for a second, and his whole body responded in kind.

No matter what their problems, the physical attraction was definitely still there, front and centre, if his trouser tent was anything to go by. He tried to think of mundane things such as folding laundry and the principles of asepsis as he sat down on the bed and handed her a plate. 'I hope you can eat pizza with your left hand.'

'It's going to be a challenge,' she admitted with a grimace. 'But trust me, I'm so hungry I'll manage one way or another. Any news on Papa?'

'Nothing yet. But I can assure you, if there was any news, good or bad, Dom would call immediately. My guess is that he's still in Theatre or Recovery.'

'Okay. Well, while we wait I may as well eat.' She picked up a piece of pizza with her left hand and, twisting her palm at a very odd angle, hooked her fingers around it. The end of the slice drooped and she dipped her head quickly to catch the dripping oil and cheese with her mouth. She ate with gusto. 'Ta-da!'

'Messy, but ten out of ten for effort.' He thought about offering to feed her, but knew that was a step beyond where they were right now.

But when she'd finished eating, he did grab a napkin, take hold of her oily hand and wipe it for her. As he did so her body seemed to relax and she smiled as she watched him. 'Thank you, Lucas. You're such a gentleman.'

'I just didn't want to get pizza oil on my fancy bedding.' He winked.

She laughed. 'No. You wanted to help me. Admit it.'

'Yes. I did. But I don't want to be overbearing.' Generally happy to be in his own company, he wasn't used to blurting out his feelings, but in this case it was important for them both to know where they stood. Their child was too important for ambiguity. 'The truth is, Giada, I'm not sure where we go from here.'

'Neither am I.' Her shoulders dipped, but she looked relieved they were actually talking. 'But you could start by calling me Gigi. Like you used to.'

'But that's a family nickname. I'm not family.'

'You called me that before.'

'Yes, when we were…' How should he put it?

'Playing?' Her eyes slid up to meet his and for the first time since they'd met earlier this afternoon he felt as if the barriers were starting to shift. She breathed out and shook her head. 'This is very difficult, *sì*?'

He nodded. 'Yes.'

'You don't want a baby.'

'I didn't. Now? It's sinking in.' But he didn't want to give her the wrong impression that they were going to walk off into the sunset together. That was, if he was even worthy of being accepted into the Royal family as some sort of… what? What exactly would he be to them? A complication? An error of judgement? Always on the outside. 'But it makes everything awkward between Dom and myself, too.'

'He'll get over it.'

'I don't think you understand how a man feels about protecting his little sister. I've broken unspoken vows. He'll kill me. What did you say the punishment was? Beheading?' He was only half joking but his relationship with Dom would be irrevocably changed and strained by this and that thought was like a low blow in his gut.

He lifted the tray from the bed and put it on the dressing table then sat down next to her again. She crossed her legs, tucking her heels under her knees. 'We are both adults, Lucas. We can do what we like. Besides, my brother hasn't been home for ten years. I can't remember him ever wanting to protect me.'

'He does, of course he does. One of the reasons he stayed here was to protect you from the fallout of him arguing with your Papa.'

She spread the fingers of her good hand and ran them through her almost dry hair, teasing out the curls into gentle waves. 'Papa does a good line in arguing, *sì*. I do love him, but he can be hard to live with. He has expectations and standards that I constantly fail.'

'Never.'

'I've been in the gossip pages for half my life and rarely for a good reason. As you can imagine, he's not a big fan of that.'

'You were forced to grow up in the spotlight. At some point you were going to stuff up.'

'Thank you for understanding.' She threw him a look of gratitude. 'He hasn't forgiven me for the things I did in the past. It feels as if he's just waiting for me to drop the ball again and drag the family into yet another scandal.' She cupped her belly with her palm. 'Looks like he's right about that. But I'm having this baby and I'm proud I'm going to be a mother.'

Pride? He hadn't thought about that particular emotion yet; he was still reeling from finding out he was going to be a father. What kind of father was he going to be? Distant, like his father had been and continued to be? No. There was no way he'd have a part of him out there in the world and not want to watch it grow up, be involved somehow.

'Sounds like neither of us exactly has a blueprint for happy families,' he said, choosing not to embellish that with his own sorry familial experiences. 'Which makes getting things right so important. I'm guessing your father doesn't know about the baby?'

'What? No! Not yet. He's had enough to deal with, with a brain tumour and surgery later in the month. And now…well he's very sick. I have to wait.'

'You are going to tell him, though? And Dom? You can't just get bigger—'

She laughed. 'Don't panic, Captain Sensible. I am going to tell them, of course. But you and I need a plan first. I'm assuming you'd want parental rights?'

'Ah, you make it sound so affirming and fluffy.' He bit back irritation, still astounded that two hours ago he'd been totally oblivious that his world was about to be tipped upside down. 'Yes, Giada. I want to be involved in my child's life.' Whatever happened, he would try to be a better father than the one he'd had.

'How? How's that going to work? I mean…' She bit her lip, frowning as if this was a very hard puzzle. 'What are your…um, intentions?'

'I don't understand.' What was she asking? 'Are you expecting…? Do we need to get married, is that what you want?'

'What? Really?' She blinked and then, surprisingly, laughed. 'Lucas Beaufort, is this a proposal?'

'Yes. Um. No. Not exactly.' He wasn't at all sure how he'd feel if she said yes.

'Good, because it needs work. No. No, Lucas. I don't *need* to marry you.' She flicked her hand towards him. 'This isn't the Dark Ages. I am perfectly capable and financially secure enough to look after this baby on my own. And by the sound of it you hate the thought of it…'

He did. At least, he had. Now, he wasn't so sure. And, hell, even though he'd had no intention of proposing or marrying her, the rejection stung.

'It's okay. We don't need make any decisions yet; we have plenty of time to figure this out. You need to sleep. We can chat more tomorrow.'

'Ah. About that…' She pressed her lips together and looked down at her good hand. 'The thing is… I'm going home tomorrow.'

'What? You've only just got here.'

'Someone from the family needs to be in Isola Verde. I've phoned my private secretary and she's arranged for a flight…scheduled, unfortunately, but it's all we can do at such short notice.'

'Wait. You've done what?' What the actual hell? He fought to keep his shock under control. Oh, she was full of surprises, Giada Baresi. 'You just went ahead and arranged that without talking to me or Dom? What about…?' He'd been going to say 'us', but there wasn't any 'us'. It was Princess Giada and Lucas Beaufort. Two separate people brought together by lust and now forced to be connected for the rest of their lives. 'Is this how it's going to be? You making all the decisions and informing me of them, and I get no say?' He couldn't live like that. 'Damn it, Giada.

I don't want control, but I do deserve an equal say in things.'

'My nation needs someone from the Royal family at home. Particularly when news breaks about Papa's accident. Dom can't go, can he? He's got to be here with our father and do his job. So it has to be me. Unfortunately, you are having a child with a princess and I have duties to perform whether you—or I—like it or not.'

She sat up and he saw the regal jaw, the tilt of her chin, the resolution in her eyes. He reminded himself that this was the indomitable and independent Princess Giada Baresi who had grown up with all the trappings of wealth, privilege and responsibility despite the occasional tongue lashing from her father, not soft, sweet Gigi who'd giggled against his naked chest and had sighed his name when she'd come.

'I am leaving tomorrow, Lucas. I have duties I have to attend to at home.' She paused. Thought for a moment. There was a tease in her eyes as she said, 'Is that okay with you?'

Well, at least she was listening.

'What would have been nicer would have been a conversation that went along the lines of…"Hey, I'm thinking I should go home. There isn't anyone else available and I think I need to be there to give some stability to the nation while the King and Crown Prince are out of the country. What do you think, Lucas?"'

'To which I could have answered, "Sure thing. That sounds like a great plan. How can I help you? Remember, you only have one active hand so you'll need extra support."' He paused to check his tone had been supportive rather than critical. 'And you could have said, "I'll be okay, Lucas, because I have people to help me, but thank you for offering."'

But even though he'd hoped she'd receive his comments well, her eyebrows rose and she looked stunned. 'You want me to ask permission before I do anything? *Dio*, you're like my papa!'

'I do not want you to ask for permission, I'd just like us to have a conversation. I'd like us to work together with this…new issue.' He looked at her, saw the confusion and, yes, anger, clouding her eyes and he knew he was stepping over the line here. 'You may well be a princess but, damn, in this house we're just a man and a woman trying to make a future that will work for us both.'

'I am always a princess, Lucas. That is something I cannot change.'

'You *have* changed, Giada.'

'You said that to me once before, Lucas, remember?' She bristled, her back straightening, her mouth flattening into a tight line. 'Only last time you said it with admiration and respect and now it just sounds bitter.'

'I'm not bitter, I'm blindsided. I'm trying to work out what we do next but you're always one step ahead of me, making your own decisions. I'm always playing catch-up. I just need a moment or two where we can talk civilly to each other.' Which was laughable because he wasn't sure how civil he could be when he wanted to kiss her again and again. She was volatile and aristocratic, fiery and unbending, but, hell, she was also sexy and surprising and beautiful.

Which, if he was honest, wasn't helping him keep his head clear and logical.

She sighed. 'Then come with me. We can talk on the plane. We can talk at the palace.'

'What? Just drop everything and travel across the world? Duck out of my job at a moment's notice? It's not that easy to leave my colleagues one member of staff down. Plus, there's an important charity event in a couple of weeks that I have to attend.'

'More chilli eating?' She threw at him with a look of scorn.

'A ball to raise money to add a new wing to the children's cancer ward at Seattle General. It's important. I have a *life* here, Giada. I have things to do, roster commitments...' He wasn't sure if she even knew what that meant. 'You have your own hospital project so you must know adequate staffing levels are always an issue. Never mind leaving Dom here to cope with your family's problems on his own.'

'He has Logan and all his ER staff around him. He can visit Papa's bedside and talk to him. Wish him better. When our father wakes up they will need time together without me being there. Papa's always better if I'm not around. And, besides, Dom's been coping without us…' she blinked and Lucas just knew she meant *without me* '…for long enough. I came here to tell you about the baby and that job is done. I need to go home.'

'And what am I supposed to do?' Follow her? Step back? If he did that he wasn't sure how involved he'd be in his child's life. He needed to make a stand now, from the beginning. Wow. His life had gone from busy yet simple to crowded and complicated in the blink of an eye. 'I understand you need to go home. Is there any way I can convince you to stay just a little bit longer so we can talk things through?'

'I have to go. I'm sorry, Lucas. I am needed. I have to be the voice of the family. You could come along later. When you have time?'

As far as he'd been concerned it would never be the right time to be a father, but he was faced with an impossible choice. Leave his job here, if only for a few days, or risk losing the first chance to make plans for a good life for his child. Time was the one thing he'd been deprived of with his own family and it was his biggest regret.

He looked at Giada. Her hair was a mess of crazy waves that stuck out at odd angles from where she'd lain on it. Her eyes were bruised with exhaustion. The slash of red across her sternum from the seatbelt was changing to purple and yellow and must hurt like hell every time she moved. Her arm was damaged and no doubt causing her a lot of pain. She needed to take some time to rest and heal but she was determined to do the right thing by the people who needed her.

She'd faced so much on her own over the years, having been left in Isola Verde without her mother or brother on side, and had risen above the hurt she'd felt from her father's criticisms. Now she was facing a royal crisis and a pregnancy that was possibly not going to be well received. And still she was determined to overcome it all, on her own.

Well, he wasn't going to let that happen.

Besides, he needed to put this child first and they needed to talk more. 'Okay. I'll make some calls and pack a bag.'

When he'd woken up this morning he'd been expecting a busy day in the ER. Not a seismic shift in his world and a sudden trip across the globe.

But if Giada Baresi was going to Isola Verde then he was going too.

CHAPTER FOUR

HE WAS IN the next room.

Was he thinking about all this the same way she was? Was his head whirling with possibilities and yet roadblocks too? What was going to happen to them all?

Was he thinking about her? About their child?

From her bed she'd heard his murmured voice in the room down the corridor as he'd talked on the phone, then she'd heard bumps and thuds. Lifting down a suitcase? And then nothing. For hours. He was probably sleeping like she should have been, but ever since her head had hit the pillow her mind had been full again, reliving the accident. Recoiling from Lucas's initial reaction to her news. His face when he'd seen their baby on the monitor.

Lucas. The only man who'd intrigued her because he'd initially rebuffed her and who hadn't been blinded by her title and riches. The only man who'd ever proposed so reluctantly it had almost made her laugh—and, yes, she had a few proposals under her belt. She almost wished she could rewind it to let him hear his tone: *I'm asking you to marry me, but please don't say yes.*

She imagined him lying on his side, dressed in his usual bed wear of…nothing. And then, just as it had so many, many times before, her mind filled with images of him. The way his eyes misted as he kissed her. The way his jaw set as he cried out her name as they climaxed together. The water droplets on his eyelashes in the sea, in the shower, in the pool. His laugh.

She'd dug deep enough to uncover the man she thought was the real Lucas Beaufort. A smiling, laughing man who was generous and funny and considerate. Who hadn't treated her as if she was in a glass cage, hadn't had any agenda but to enjoy her and to give her enjoyment. She couldn't remember the last man who'd been interested in her and not just her title. Oh, and he was as sexy as hell.

Her body tingled with a keen low ache, hot and needy, to be with him again.

Was he thinking about her the way she was thinking about him? Did he want her the way her body longed for his?

Was he thinking about her naked? About that weekend when they'd taken and given so much, exploring each other, tasting.

She could taste him now.

Stupido. He'd made it clear he was coming to Isola Verde because he had to, not because he wanted to. So lying here all hot and turned on wasn't going to help her one tiny bit.

Time to get real. It was okay, she could weather this storm on her own the way she'd weathered all the others. She didn't need anyone. She could cope perfectly well on her own. And, yes, single parenting would be hard but compared to most solo mothers she was in a far better position— or she would be once she'd explained it all to her family.

There was the sticking point. Her courage wobbled.

Giada sat up, checked her phone. A text from Dom saying their father was out of surgery and being kept in a coma but responding well. Stable.

That was good. And a lot more than she felt right now.

The airport staff couldn't do enough for her…a first-class customer who'd insisted on anonymity and got it. And somehow they'd wrangled Lucas to be upgraded to first class too, so they could sit together for twelve hours. They could talk then. He still wasn't sure what he was going to say.

He'd had to help reinstate the sling this morning, if only to remind her not to use her sore wrist. The bruising across her chest had bloomed overnight and she was walking as if every step caused her pain, but she didn't ask for help and didn't complain. Not once.

The first-class lounge was next level. Sure, Lucas flew business class when he could, but this was something else with its glittering chandeliers and hushed-voice staff.

Finally, after an early start where they'd only managed rudimentary conversation in the cab that had brought them to the airport, they were alone and able to chat. Giada smiled warily as soon as the lounge waitress finished serving them a hot breakfast of scrambled eggs and salad.

'Lucas, I know this is difficult for you, but thank you for taking time off. Did Dom ask any difficult questions when you called him? I'm hoping you didn't mention our news?'

'I didn't call Dom. He's the head of the ER, sure, but I need to clear any leave with HR. I had time owing. Hell, we all have time owing. God knows what would happen if we all decided to take it together. I said I knew Dom was busy and asked them to pass on my apologies to him and told them I needed to take time off immediately for personal and family reasons.'

He laughed at the irony of that and wondered what conclusion Dom would come to. He only hoped his best friend was too distracted by work and his sick father to put two and two together about his sister and colleague going AWOL on the same day. 'I don't feel great about not keeping him in the loop.'

If this had just been about him he'd have fronted up to his friend and explained, but it wasn't just about him, and his life wouldn't just be about him ever again.

'He'll understand, eventually.'

'Somehow I doubt that.' He'd left Dom in the lurch and short-staffed, instead of being there for his friend at a very difficult and stressful time. He'd need to do a lot of grovelling when he finally saw his mate face to face again. Swallowing his guilt, Lucas watched as Giada tried to eat her breakfast one-handed, stabbing at it unenthusiastically. 'You need to eat more than that.'

'I'm really not hungry.' With her fork in her left hand she rolled a halved cherry tomato across a slick of pesto sauce. 'One thing I've learnt is that morning sickness doesn't just happen in the morning, and even though the books say it should stop around twelve weeks, it doesn't.'

God, he hadn't even thought about that. Her body was undergoing changes and she was dealing with all that plus the accident, and now shouldering responsibility for her nation's welfare. 'Let me cut it up for you.'

Her eyes met his, her tone sharp. 'I can manage.'

So they were back to awkward conversation again. Great. His morning wasn't going well.

Luckily, they were interrupted by a staff member. 'Excuse me, Your Highness, they're calling your flight now. Time to go to the gate.'

Your Highness. Too often he forgot that. To him she was Gigi, but to everyone else in the world she was on a pedestal, out of reach, to be observed and commented on. He was utterly out of his depth here.

'Okay. Thank you— Oh. My phone's ringing.' Giada stood up but paused, her eyes panic-stricken as she looked at the screen. 'It's Dom. We don't have time, but what if there's news?'

'Take it. They'll wait for their VIP passengers.' And, wow, that felt strange. Their lives were so completely different and he'd have to straddle it all.

He picked up her carry-on luggage and watched as she spoke to her brother, telling him she was going home, apologising for the abruptness of it and for not warning him of their visit in the first place. Clearly Dom was surprised at this sudden turnabout and it didn't start out as a positive conversation, but she did a fair amount of pacifying and explaining. Someone needed to be in Isola Verde and she was the only real choice, but as they chatted the initial tension across her shoulders eventually eased until she finished off with, 'I miss you, too.' She didn't mention Lucas.

Finally, she flicked her phone off as another call for their flight was issued, and sighed. 'Papa's still stable. Still in a coma. No change. Which I guess is good news.'

'Absolutely.' He took her arm.

'One thing…they had to operate on his brain overnight. What does "intracranial pressure is under control" mean?' Worry lines etched her face, making her look beautiful but vulnerable, and his heart shifted to make space for this woman who was trying to be everything to everyone.

'It means they're monitoring the pressure in his brain. Often it rises if there's an injury and the brain swells, or if there's bleeding or a tumour.'

'He has a tumour already, so a bleed could make things so much worse, right?'

'Max Granger operated as soon as he arrived yesterday to release the pressure so I'd say he's in very good hands, Giada.'

'I know, I do and I'm so, so grateful, especially to Max because he wasn't scheduled to come over for the tumour surgery until the fifteenth of December. It's just hard to leave them. I wish I could stay, I want to. I want to be there when Papa wakes up, I want to be there by my brother's side, but… I can't. One of us has to be at home.'

She smiled hesitantly, looking for reassurance, which he gave her with a nod rather than tell her all the things that could go wrong in her father's recovery from the accident and his brain tumour from now on. She needed his support and that was what he was going to give her. She looked so vulnerable he wanted to wrap her in his arms and make her feel safe, or better, or…something. Instead, he fell into step with her towards the departure gate.

'You're doing the right thing.' He actually had no idea if she was…he couldn't imagine what the right thing was in this situation, but she was following her heart and her royal instincts and he had to make sure she felt supported in that.

She nodded. 'And Dom said he misses me.'

'I told you he would. If not for the accident, this time in Seattle would have been a good chance for you to get to know each other again.'

'We've communicated more in the last couple of days than we have in months. I just wish it was under better circumstances.' She gave Lucas an uncertain smile at the use of his words from yesterday and she softened a little, her good hand on his arm. 'Once we know what our plan is we'll talk to him, okay? I don't want you to feel bad about your friendship because of me.'

'I own this, Giada. This is on me, just as much as you. It takes two. We're in this together.'

'Thank you.' She blinked up at him then, her beautiful eyes shimmering, and he realised just how much she'd been hoping for that kind of re-action to her news. He could see how desperately she wanted him to be happy about the baby while all along he'd been thinking only about how all this affected him and his life and relationships. Yeah. Great. Selfish jerk.

He swiped his ticket in the machine at the gate and started to walk towards the front of the plane, but a buzzing in his pocket made him stop. He looked at his phone. Dom. *Damn*. Normally, Lucas would be straight onto speaking with his friend, but he let it go to voicemail.

Guilt rippled through him. He was being a lousy employee and a lousy friend so he had to make sure he was a damned good father.

The flight was long and even though he tried to talk to Giada, the engine sounds, the spacing of their seats and the staff attentiveness meant it just wasn't an ideal time or place for the kind of con-versation they needed. And since Giada slept, he tried to do the same.

When the aircraft started its descent, he looked out of the window for his first glimpse of Giada's home: a large island of green in the sparkling deep blue Mediterranean Sea. He knew from both Giada and Dom that it was a fertile land producing an array of fruit and vegetables bursting with flavour and freshness. From this height he could see olive groves and lemon orchards and, as they swooped low on their airport trajectory, hillsides festooned in vines.

He was also surprised to see a smattering of high-rise tower blocks bearing the names of global accounting companies, indicating a modern, vibrant kingdom with a respectable economy and, in the distance was a shimmering white building on the top of a hill surrounded by acres of greenery. Glittering marble painted orange by the sunset. The palace. Giada's home.

His heart started to race. What was in store for him here? How would he be a father to a baby who would grow up here?

He barely had time to think before they were bustled off the plane and through the private exit door at Isola Verde International Airport to be greeted by a woman who looked to be in her early forties, wearing a navy blue trouser suit and standing in front of one of the royal fleet of cars with a small purple and silver flag sticking out of the badge on the bonnet. Well, wow.

Giada greeted the woman with a warm handshake. '*Ciao*, Maria!'

The woman dipped a curtsey with Giada's hand clasped in hers and replied in Isola Verdian.

Lucas coughed. Wow again. A curtsey. He

hadn't even thought about that. Giada turned to glance at him, a smile hovering on her lips, before she addressed the woman in English, he suspected for his benefit. 'This is Lucas Beaufort. He'll be staying with us for a little while.'

'Of course, ma'am.' The woman nodded to Lucas and shook his extended hand. 'Welcome to Isola Verde, Mr Beaufort.'

'*Dr* Beaufort,' Giada interjected. 'Lucas, this is Maria, my private secretary and all-round wing woman.'

Lucas nodded. 'Hello.'

'Ah. Your arm, ma'am?' Maria asked, her face creasing in concern as she looked at the sling. 'You needed a doctor to travel with you. Is it bad?'

But Giada laughed. 'It's not broken. I'm fine. Lucas is here as my guest, not as my doctor. We're keeping his visit low-key. As in let's not mention it to my brother should he call.'

'Understood, ma'am.' Maria opened the car door for Giada to get in and was about to do the same for Lucas but he shook his head and motioned for her to get into the driver's seat. He walked round to the other side of the car and settled Giada into her seat, making sure the seatbelt went over the undamaged part of her collarbone and carefully cradled her belly.

'Lucas,' she whispered, 'I'm not made of porcelain, I'm not going to break.'

But even so, he could see the gratitude in her eyes for his care.

'Let's just be careful, okay? Precious cargo.' Wanting to touch his hand to her belly right there, to feel the life inside her, to protect it from any ensuing danger, he quickly swallowed and leaned across her, snapping the seatbelt in place, telling himself it was simply because she'd struggle to do it with her sore arm. But as he stretched back across her their eyes met.

He was momentarily frozen by the intensity of her gaze. The warm dark brown that had danced with carefree joy three months ago was now filled with concern and confusion. Nevertheless, even in this state her gaze took him back to the beach, to that teasing manner and her insistence they play. To that first touch of her lips.

His eyes lingered over her mouth. She licked her bottom lip and desire shot through him like a bolt of electricity.

She felt it too, he could see. Saw the flare of desire, watched as the wall of aloofness she'd been cloaked in since they'd got up that morning start to crumble.

'Lucas.' Another whisper against his neck.

He jerked his hand from her thigh where it had rested after he'd clipped the seatbelt then took his place next to her, shaken to the core by the intensity not just of desire but of…*emotion*. Something about this woman made him want to protect her, to let down his guard. It wasn't just the fact she was having his baby, it was more than that…it was her endearing desire to do the right thing, to put on a brave face, to carry everyone's burden, all mixed up with the playful woman he'd known three months ago, the one who'd accepted him, flaws and all, the woman he wanted to find again.

But going back to that would be impossible. He clipped on his seatbelt and vowed to keep a tight hold on his self-control for the rest of the trip.

Giada concentrated on being a tour guide instead of dwelling on the desire washing through her at his touch. She'd been too aware of the press of his hand on her thigh, the way his scent filled the car, the gravity of his gaze that was at once forbidding and enticing.

He was struggling with all of this; they both were. But here in Isola Verde she was the host and the Princess, and she'd have to work out the problem that was her attraction to Lucas and the connection that sparked whenever she looked at him.

They drove first through the old town of narrow streets and cobblestones that were as familiar to her as breathing. She watched his face as he took in the ancient buildings and vibrant marketplace bustling with activity. Loved the way his eyes lit up at the pretty marina and the children playing soccer in the street, dodging traffic and laughing as if they had no cares in the world.

Ah, *bella* Isola Verde. Even with everything clashing in her head and her heart, it felt good to be home and for the millionth time in her life she wondered, with a sharp pain stabbing her chest, how Domenico could have stayed away for so long.

She busied herself pointing out places of interest, wanting Lucas to see the beauty she saw here, wanting him to fall in love with the place the way she loved it. Wanting him to fall in love with their baby, too. She wanted him to fall—

No.

Her heart hammered at the direction her mind had taken. Falling in love with Lucas was not her plan. They were too different, had too many issues to overcome—wanting anything long term was completely irrational. She'd armoured her heart against getting involved with another man. Vowed to keep everyone at an emotional arm's length, the way her father had taught her, the way he'd lived. No show of emotion, no attachment. Cool and distant.

And, okay, she couldn't do cool and distant because she liked fun too much—she had far too much of her mother's DNA not to make the best of everything—but being broken and burnt had also taught her to keep her heart out of any romantic adventure ever again.

Her people had started decorating the buildings for Christmas with heavy, colourful garlands strung between the houses and across the narrow streets. Some of the shop windows already had nativity displays with miniature statues of the baby in the manger watched over by sparkling silver angels. One thing Isola Verde did really well was Christmas. She just hoped it would be a happy one for them all, hoped her father would be recovered and well for another year of his reign. And hoped Dom would have come to terms with his destiny.

'This part of the city is almost nine hundred years old. We can trace our family right back to the birth of our nation when the first Alessandro arrived here from Rome, claiming the island as his and declaring himself Alessandro the First. He built the cathedral.' She pointed to a magnificent marble building built in the black and white style of Florence's Duomo and felt a punch of pride for her country and its history.

'Later, his grandson opened the first real school here. We have an excellent education system and the Royal family have been both benefactors and beneficiaries of it. Both Dom and I went to school here. Obviously, Papa gave Domenico permission to go to medical school in the States, but I…well, let's say I just about scraped through the Isola Verde version of the Baccalaureate. Traditionally, Royal children stay on the island for their schooling…'

She left the rest of the sentence hanging. It was expected that Royal children go to school here but how would Lucas respond to that? He'd said they needed to talk and that she had to consult him, which was fair, but what about ancient traditions and protocol?

'I see.' His eyebrows rose. 'I went to my local school too, as did my brother and sister. Then to Downing College, Cambridge. It's expected that all Beauforts go there, too.'

'I see.' She echoed his own response. 'I know Cambridge is an excellent university. Did you all study the same thing? Are you descended from a long line of doctors the way I'm descended from a long line of royalty?'

'No.' Something crossed his face, a shadow of pain. Then it was gone with a shake of his head. 'But I'd like to think my child could choose their own path.'

'Sometimes you don't get a choice about who you are.' But there was truth in what he was saying. Dom had railed against the path that had been forced upon him from birth and look where that had got them—barely seeing him for over a decade, a dash across the world, a skid on black ice and a lot of heartache. But there was something else in Lucas's words that jarred. 'Didn't you want to study medicine?'

'On the contrary, medicine was all I ever wanted to do.'

'I don't understand what you're saying.'

'It isn't always in a child's best interests to have their future mapped out for them. Even a royal prince or princess.'

Her eyes darted to Maria and she lowered her voice. Her secretary was completely discreet, always, but there were some things she wasn't ready to share. Yet. 'You're referring to Dom?'

'I'm referring to experience.'

'Lucas, I don't understand. What happened?'

He shook his head and looked out of the window. 'It's of no consequence, Giada. Only, hypothetically speaking, if I ever *were* to have a child...' he glanced at Maria '... I would need to have an equal say in where it went to school. As would the child.'

'Okay. Right. Good to know. I'll take your opinion into account.'

'You'll do more than that.' He glared at her.

Giada bristled with frustration. Controlling her irritation and disappointment, she raised her voice. 'Maria, straight to the palace, please.'

CHAPTER FIVE

HOW WERE THEY going to navigate the rest of their child's life if they couldn't even agree on one simple thing?

But, then, none of this was simple. Lucas was already too aware of that. Trying to swallow the frustration emanating through him, he climbed out of the car and gaped at the huge glittering stone and marble *palace*.

The argument melted from his mind as he took in the scale of the place, the breathtaking beauty and purity of the white stone and the striking regal purple and silver flag that fluttered proudly in the unexpectedly warm breeze.

He hadn't been sure what to expect but the palace and its grounds were beyond anything he'd imagined. A grand tree-lined avenue opened to a central three-storey building with a stepped roof and ornate central green dome. Spreading out east and west from the centre dome were large angled wings, two, as far as he could see, but possibly more. He lost count of the number of windows…too many, so many, indicating a labyrinth of rooms and corridors inside.

'It's…' he ran a hand through his hair and shook his head, lost for words all over again '…magnificent.'

Giada gave him a side-eye. 'Oh, you know, it's a bit cramped but it'll do.'

'How many rooms?'

'Two hundred and thirty-two.' She laughed. 'But you don't have to visit them all. Most of them are dull anyway, just formal state rooms and galleries. Don't worry about your bags, Paulo will carry them up for you.'

Lucas grimaced, unsure how he felt about having people to do his bidding. 'I can manage my own bag, Giada.'

'Very well. It's up to you, of course. I've asked Maria to put you in the Napoli suite. You should be comfortable there.'

He wasn't sure he'd be comfortable anywhere here. Sure, it was luxurious but…overwhelmingly huge. 'How do you ever find your way around?'

'You learn. Places you can go, places you can't. There are shortcuts, corridors, secret tunnels.' She winked, clearly more relaxed to be in familiar surroundings. Their clash about schooling was still a bruise in his memory. They would come back to it eventually, along with all the other things they'd need to discuss, including things he no doubt hadn't even thought of yet. But for now he needed to get his bearings.

As if she'd read his mind, she smiled. 'I'll give you a tour later. First, I have a couple of meetings I need to get to. I'll be back for dinner.'

'You have meetings now? You've been on the go since dawn. When are you going to rest, Giada?'

'I slept on the flight. Well, a little.' Her eyes were edged with shadows, but her smile was warm and grateful at his words as if she'd been waiting, again, for him to show he cared about the baby. 'Okay. I'll make sure I rest later, I promise. After the meetings. I need to brief the staff and we need to make a statement about the accident. It's not right to keep secrets for too long: you always get found out in the end.'

He knew that well enough.

'Ah, here's Paulo. He'll show you to your room.' She said something in Isola Verdian to the uniformed young man who gave a low bow. The man nodded and turned, clipping his heels together, and indicated for Lucas to follow him. Giada patted his arm. 'Feel free to explore. The gardens are amazing.' She was swept away by Maria, ascending the white stone steps two at a time, and then she was swallowed up by the huge building.

And, before he had a chance to look at his

surroundings, he was whisked through a security system exactly like the one at the airport, complete with X-ray machine, up a set of stairs, through myriad doors and corridors to his suite.

He stood for a moment, taking it all in—a drawing room, bedroom, bathroom and modern kitchen, all beautifully decorated with a mix of period furniture and contemporary features like a huge TV, internet modem and surround speaker system.

All very nice, but where did Giada live? Was she close to here? Where was her suite? Did she need his help?

Then he smiled to himself at the memory of her playful expression when she'd mentioned secret corridors. He'd bet she'd had fun navigating them when she was younger.

Ah, Giada. *Gigi*. His heart twisted. Why was this all so damned complicated?

After showering, he dressed in casual jeans and a shirt, choosing clothes more suitable for a temperate winter than his thick Seattle coat and boots.

And waited.

No one came and no one rang, so he decided to explore. Hell, it wasn't as if he stayed in a palace every day. He ventured down a sweeping staircase and couldn't help whistling in admiration at the vast entrance hall with a painted fresco on the roof that he was pretty sure was frosted in real gold. Everywhere he turned he saw artwork from famous artists he'd actually heard of, bronzes, statues and porcelains on plinths. There was even a huge marble fountain with a statue of a Roman god in the centre that would have filled up the whole square footage, and more, of the first floor of his Denny-Blaine house.

He lost count of the number of uniformed staff who passed him and nodded their welcome; some spoke a greeting in English, some in Isola Verdian. No one questioned who he was or why he was there—it felt as if everyone had been informed of his presence.

He stopped to admire not one, not two but three real Christmas trees in the hallway that must have been ten feet tall but still reached nowhere near the height of the dome. Decadently decorated in purple and silver garlands and festooned with tiny fairy lights, they would have given the Seattle General Hospital's famous festive tree display a run for its money, never mind his scrappy and woeful plastic tree he hadn't even bothered to get out last year. The smell was divine and threw him back to happy times with his family. Before…

Once upon a time he'd exceeded their expectations. And now they didn't even know where he was. In a palace! Go figure. How would his parents react to the news they were going to be grandparents? Would he tell them? Would they care?

His head suddenly swam with images of a toddler sitting here, opening presents. Christmas was never going to be the same. Would he even get to see his child for the holidays?

Damn sure he would.

When he reached the huge wooden iron-studded front door he was stopped by a security guard. '*Mi scusi*, Dr Beaufort?'

'Yes, I'm Dr Beaufort. Is it okay for me to go out of here? And, more importantly, will I be able to get back in?'

'Of course, sir. You have security clearance. Wait, please.' He ducked into an office and came out brandishing a card on a lanyard. 'Here's your swipe card and ID.'

ID for walking around a house? How would he ever get used to this? How would his child?

He imagined growing up here in such opulence, with such gravitas and history. With the weight of responsibility always, *always* at the forefront of your mind. Being separate from everyone, being observed and scrutinised the way Giada had been all her life. He didn't want that for his child. He wanted normality—whatever that was. He wanted the freedom he had been given…and he wanted…yes, he wanted to be a better parent than his had been.

He followed a gravel path round to the rear of the building, meandering through a walled kitchen garden stuffed with blooming winter vegetables that gave onto the colourful *parterre* complete with the fountain he could see from his suite. Then a more formal garden with neatly clipped boxwood hedges and perfectly groomed lawns. Wanting to stretch his legs after the long flight and trying to get his thoughts in order, he walked through a copse of beech trees and found a secluded lake he hadn't seen from the palace. The fading orange light dappled and danced on the water and he inhaled deeply, finally able to breathe and think. Some peace to gather his thoughts.

He bent and swished his hand in the water… nowhere near as cold or as large as his lake at home. He hadn't actually ventured back into the lake at the bottom of his Seattle garden because swimming just hadn't been the same since his Gigi weekend. He smiled. She'd been spectacular then, glistening with water, nipples erect from cold but hot to his touch. The lust from before, when he'd skimmed his hands over her thighs, hit him again and it became very clear that when it came to Giada he couldn't be objective, at least not when it came to physical attraction.

And, yeah, it seemed like his thoughts were hell-bent on turning to her over and over and over.

'I wondered if I'd find you out here. It's one of my favourite places too.'

'What the—?' He turned quickly, heart rattling, and almost lost his footing. He waved his arms about to right himself and found himself face to face with the Princess. 'God, Giada, you made me jump.'

'Sorry.' She laughed. She'd changed out of her travelling clothes and was now wearing a form-fitting deep orange buttoned-up cashmere cardigan that hugged her amazing curves and cream trousers that nipped in slightly at her ankles. Her hair was loose, curls gracing her shoulders. Her face had been scrubbed clean of make-up and she looked fresher but still tired. Her injured wrist was supported in an inexpert sling almost as badly fashioned as his original effort, but she reached out her good hand to steady him. 'You looked so peaceful I almost didn't say anything. For a minute there I thought you might take a dip.'

He pretended to shiver, even though the weather was mild. In truth, he was just trying to steady his heart as it pounded, not just from the shock of surprise but from the shock of seeing her. She made his body react every time he set eyes on her. 'I'm used to cold water, but even

I won't swim in December. How did the meetings go?'

'Good.' She nodded decisively as if trying to convince herself that everything was okay, but how could it be with the uncertainty of her father's condition? 'We're working with the new PR director at Seattle Hospital, Ayanna Franklin, to keep his location a secret. The plan is to release a statement that is honest but vague, mentioning a car accident and that Papa is stable and in good hands and that we're praying for a speedy recovery. I'm preparing myself for the onslaught of questions.'

'Do you have to answer them?'

'Journalists constantly reach out to our press office, more so at times like this, and I feel I have a duty to eliminate as much ambiguity as I can. And there's social media, of course, where everyone expresses an opinion. It's hard not to see, difficult not to look. The comments sections are always…illuminating. Not always complimentary, to be honest. Not towards the office or the King, who is revered here, but most definitely not towards things I have done in the past.' She shook her head, the light in her eyes dimming a little. 'If we don't keep abreast of what people are thinking and feeling, we lose touch. Our staff bring the relevant questions and comments for us to digest and respond.'

He'd never heard Dom talk about digesting people's opinions about the kingdom; his friend had appeared to be consumed only by study and work. But who knew how closely the Prince had followed life in Isola Verde, albeit from a distance? It felt as if his friend's life had been lived half in the light and half veiled. Unless, of course, her brother had chosen not to participate in any of this. Lucas felt a sudden sting of irritation for the lack of support from anyone close to her. 'You shouldn't have to deal with this on your own, Giada.'

Her back stiffened. 'I have Maria and my father's advisors.'

'But you still look at the comments, right?'

'Sometimes, but if I don't like what everyone's saying I look through my fingers,' she admitted, putting her hands in front of her face and pulling a pretend scared expression.

But Lucas felt unfathomably protective about this. Even though she was a grown woman, he had ten years' life experience on her. He had no qualms about not even bothering with social media. It didn't matter a jot to him, plus he was a doctor and had been taught how to deal with difficult and delicate situations. Despite having been groomed to be in the public eye, Giada was vulnerable now. She shouldn't have to be anxious about reading things in the media; she shouldn't read it, full stop. 'You need a shield from all that.'

'Oh?' She gave him a wry smile. 'Are you offering?'

Why not? He could be a stand-in for her brother. Protect her from the barrage of questions she couldn't answer. He made a spur-of-the-moment decision. 'For as long as I'm here I will read the comments and will only let you read the *relevant* ones. That is, the good ones.'

She tutted. 'That's like only reading the good reviews for a book. It doesn't give you the full picture.'

'To be honest, Giada, the only thing I care about right now is keeping the baby safe and well, which means keeping you well too.' He couldn't help but glance at her belly and was swamped by a tenderness that shocked him. Yes, he would be the shield.

'Thank you. You have no idea how much that means to me. To us.' She put her good hand on her abdomen and it took all his self-control not to cover her hand with his. To feel the growing baby there. His baby. His lifeblood. He wasn't sure he was ever going to get used to that idea. 'Lucas, we have a lot to discuss and a lot to work through, so can we try to get along? I know this situation is difficult for you and you didn't ask for any of this. But we're here now and we have to make the best of it. I don't know how to navigate any of it, but I promise I'll try to take your feelings and opinions into account, if you could try to do the same.'

She was extending an olive branch, quite apt given the plethora of olive groves they'd flown over on this lush island.

Her smile turned a little wary and he hated it that their argument earlier had made her feel as if she had to tiptoe around things—he much preferred spiky, feisty Gigi. That woman made him laugh, made his heart tug, made him hot.

Which was not appropriate right now, even though his body seemed to have other ideas. He nodded. 'I'll certainly try.'

'Me too. Good.' Her smile returned. 'And I don't want to pry, but I had a feeling in the car that something had hurt you. Something to do with schooling or college. Can I ask…? Can you explain what you meant when you alluded to having had your future mapped out?'

He wasn't going there. Not today. Not ever, if he could help it. 'It's not important.'

She touched his arm. 'Lucas, it is. I can see it is. We had a fight over it. Please tell me so I can understand. What happened?'

He cursed under his breath. He wasn't going to open that wound. 'It's—'

'Look, can we be open with each other? Please? I need to know where I stand with you.'

He frowned at her words. 'What do you mean?'

'I am a princess, surely you understand that I have my "yes" people who only ever agree to my requests, no matter how crazy they are, and also people who try to wheedle their way into my favour so they can get something from me... kudos, a favour, *money*.' Her cheeks reddened and she almost spat the last word out. She softened a little. 'But you're none of these things, Lucas. I get a sense of honesty from you. I know I make mistakes, I know I'm hasty and spontaneous and I've been trying to curb that. You'll call me on my failings. In fact, you already have. Can we keep it that way?'

He liked it that she was back to being direct. 'Of course.'

'So tell me why our child's schooling is particularly important to you.'

He blew out a deep breath, hesitating as he fished around for the right words.

'I'm afraid I'm not going to be a good parent.' The admission steamed out of him before he could hold it back.

Her eyes met his and she frowned as if trying to work him out. 'Nobody knows what kind of parent they'll be. I mean, look at me. A reformed rebel princess! I have no clue about babies, but

I'll learn. *We*'ll learn. You want to do the right thing and that's the most important thing. I can't tell you how relieved I am that you care.'

He cared about the baby…that was an instinctive thing. But, he realised, he cared about Giada too, cared that she was supported and looked after. Which was a revelation considering he'd tried not to care about anyone…not deeply, not with any kind of emotional entanglement that would inevitably cost him dearly.

But there was something about Gigi that nudged and pushed and coaxed the caring side of him out of the darkest recesses of his heart. It wasn't just because of the baby she was carrying, it was her. Her sense of duty, her laughter, her gratitude. The determination to make this difficult situation work between them, no matter how unconventional…and the fact she saw the good in him.

'I had no role model, Giada. My father wasn't exactly the warm, fuzzy type.' Lucas shook his head, realising she'd prised out the thing that was haunting him most. And now, judging by her concerned and interested expression, he had to explain. 'Basically, he had plans for me and I had no say in them. I come from a family of lawyers and it was assumed I'd follow suit regardless of any dreams I had of my own. Same college, same firm, same pattern for every Beaufort for the last hundred years. Except that wasn't what I wanted to do. I didn't want to be a lawyer just because someone else had decided I should be.'

'So what happened?'

'When I told him to stuff his archaic plans and chose my own course, my parents broke off all contact with me beyond the bare minimum. A Christmas card here, a brief, emotionless text there. But after medical school, when I moved over to the States from England, it seemed to be the impetus for them to just stop answering my calls. We haven't spoken in years. I tried at first. I called. I emailed but…nothing. It's as if I don't exist. They're just not interested and have cut me out of their lives.'

Her hand went to her chest as she frowned. '*Dio*, that's awful.'

'You learn to live with it.' It had taken a long time for the sting of rejection to diminish and yet talking about it rubbed the wound raw again. His heart ached anew. 'So don't ever talk to me about happy families, because I've yet to find one.'

'Well I'm hardly a poster child for that either.' Gigi sighed. 'I think my father would gladly have cut ties with me if he could have.' She laughed, but then her face fell as she looked at him. 'They really stopped answering your calls?'

'Pretty decent parenting skills, right?'

'Oh, Lucas.' Her eyes roved his face and he

was fairly sure she blinked quickly to stem a tear or two.

But the last thing he needed was her pity. That wasn't why he'd exposed his past like a raw nerve. He started to follow the gravel path back towards the beech copse. 'It's fine. Their loss.'

'Absolutely. They're missing out. I wish they could see you now. Look at you.' Her eyes blazed with passion. He assumed it was about the way he'd been treated, but there was something else there too. Admiration maybe. A readiness to fight for him. 'You're a fine man. A good doctor.'

'With bad sling skills.' He stepped in front of her and straightened the white bandage that cut across her décolletage. She'd managed to twist the sling and the support wasn't enough to raise the wrist to the correct angle. The bruising on her chest was all yellows and purples and he winced at what this perfect body had endured. When he was satisfied the sling was giving the appropriate support he stepped back. 'But improving.'

'Every day.' She wiggled her bruised fingers as she smiled, and he was shaken by the thrum of need that zipped through his body, sharp and electric. As if every nerve ending fired into life, straining to touch her.

You can't improve on perfect. 'Recovery's going to take some time, so don't go rushing to do things. Remember to ask for help if you need it, especially with the sling.'

'Yes, Dr Beaufort,' she said in a playful, sing-song voice. 'Seriously, all I did was shower and dress. Maria helped me fix the sling.'

'Tomorrow I'll do it.'

'Do what? The sling…?' Her eyes glittered and she was back to the fun young woman who he'd made love to at the lake. 'Or the shower?'

Oh, God. He thought of her naked, covered only in suds and his hands.

Princess. Out of reach. Ten-year age gap. Bro code. He swallowed. One of them needed to stop these sparks flickering into life. 'I meant the sling, of course. It needs more support at the elbow.'

'Pity.' She held his gaze for a second. Two. More.

Her clear brown eyes simmered with heat that stoked a fire deep inside him. He was hit with an intense need to touch her again and without thinking he stepped closer. Her floral perfume mingled with the evening scents of sun-kissed wild thyme and eucalyptus. Her eyes misted. Her breathing quickened, as if she was also affected by the same shiver in the atmosphere that pulled them closer.

As he looked at her everything stilled, both around him and inside him. His gaze swept over her, over the lips he ached to kiss, the swollen breasts, the changing curves. Here, in the dappled light, she was astonishingly beautiful and utterly perfect.

She blinked up at him, desire in her eyes. Her hair was so lush and shiny, and he remembered the feel of it as it had run through his fingers. Wanting to feel it again, he reached out and slid his hands into her hair.

She covered one of his hands with hers. 'Lucas...' Her voice was cracked and the way she said his name sent arrows of need through him.

She stepped closer. Tilted her face until her mouth was mere inches away. If he dipped his head...he could kiss her again. That mouth. Her taste.

His heart thumped against his ribcage as he trailed his fingers through her hair and across to her cheek. The soft skin under his fingertips was warm but her gaze burned hot and he dipped his head. Closer.

There were so many reasons to stop, but he didn't want to. In fact, desire seemed to propel him closer.

Then she went up on tiptoe and brushed her lips against his.

Oh, God. He couldn't keep away, but he had to try. Crossing this line would only confuse things further. 'Is this the point where I call you out for being spontaneous?' he ground out against her ear.

'It's not spontaneous if you discuss it first,' she whispered, laughing as her mouth grazed his jaw.

They had a chance, then, to stop it. He should have fought, should have stepped away, but all the confusion and emotion of the last few hours coalesced inside him. She was Princess Giada. Gigi, the best lover he'd ever had. She was bearing his child. She was sexy and beautiful, and she understood he was struggling with this mindblowing craving. Understood him.

'Do it, Lucas.'

Unable to resist any longer, he crushed his mouth against hers.

'Yes.' She moaned against his lips and opened her mouth to let him in. It started as a sweet, gentle exploration. He wanted to relearn her, discover her all over again, this new Gigi who was lush and glowing and growing. She tasted the same and yet different. Fresh, sweet, addictive.

He cupped her face, relishing the feel of her soft skin under his fingertips, the sway of her body as she pressed closer to him, fitting her body against his.

Then she wound her slingless arm around his neck and deepened the kiss with heavy breaths and throaty moans, and something inside him became undone. All his self-control, all the emotions he'd been stuffing deep inside him exploded into a need he'd never experienced before. He wanted her. Wanted to be inside her again.

She spiked her fingers into his hair, dragging nails across his scalp. '*Dio*, Lucas. This is crazy, but I can't stop.'

'I… God, Gigi.' A single *no* flitted into his brain and then blurred as he propelled her backwards towards a tree and pressed her up against the bark. He slid his hand under the hem of her cardigan and up to her breast, palming her lace bra. Her breasts were fuller, bigger, even more amazing.

She shivered against him, pressing his hand hard over her nipple. '*Dio. Dio. Dio.* Lucas, don't stop.'

He started to pop open the buttons, pressing kisses down her throat, and then he saw the bruises again…she was damaged. Hurting. He imagined the pain and trauma she'd been through and pressed his mouth as gently as he could over the yellow and purple marks. 'Giada. I'm sorry—'

'I'm okay. It's okay.' She cupped his face and tugged him up to look at her, her eyes swimming with affection and desire. 'Make me feel something good instead of all this pain.'

He covered her mouth again with his, finding the one thing he hadn't realised he'd been missing for the last three months.

This.

Her.

It was almost too much. He closed his eyes. 'I didn't think this was going to happen again.'

'You think too much.' She laughed, throwing her head back, revealing the pale white of her throat.

'We should—'

'And you talk too much.' She sucked in his bottom lip. 'Kiss me instead.'

'I was actually going to say we should go somewhere more comfortable.' In truth, those words had not been in his mind. He'd been ready to stop. But looking at her, listening to her, touching her…he wanted it all.

'I like it here. Fancy some skinny dipping?' She reached for his trouser belt, playing with the buckle, a wicked glint in her eye. 'I know how much you like doing that.'

Every sensible idea was being pushed from his brain with every touch of her fingers. 'I want to taste you again.'

Her eyes widened. 'Where?'

'Everywhere.'

'Do it.'

He didn't need to be told twice. There was no need for timidity. He didn't need to relearn her, he knew what she liked, what turned her on. They were back to where they'd left off three months ago. Hungry for each other, never being sated. He pressed his mouth to her throat as he skimmed his hand around her back and undid her bra. He groaned as first his fingers then his mouth found her nipple. He sucked in the darkened, hard nub, making her writhe against him.

'*Oddio*, Lucas. Yes.' She cupped his erection.

'Gigi—' Sudden vibrations shook the ground as something thundered through the trees.

She jerked back, swiping the back of her hand across her mouth, shoulders heaving. 'What the hell?'

Sensing imminent danger, he wrapped his arm around her and pushed her behind him as the thundering got louder and louder. He felt her shiver against his back. 'It's okay, Gigi. I've got you.'

She made a funny noise as the vibrations started to lessen and the thunder died away so he turned and wrapped her close in his arms and held her tight, vowing not to let anything harm either her or her child. Ever.

But her shoulders shook and she stepped back to look up at him. He realised then that she wasn't crying in panic but laughing.

'I'm thinking the end of the world's about to happen and yet you're laughing. What's so funny?'

'It's just someone out riding, probably exercising my father's horses.' She looked down then, biting her bottom lip, sadness clouding those beautiful eyes. 'He usually rides them here or along the beach when he can. Will he ever be able to ride his horses again, Lucas?'

Reality seeped into Lucas's blurry kiss-addled brain and he stepped away, shaking himself out of the spell they'd been under with just a look. With a taste.

He shouldn't be kissing her. Not here, not again. Not ever. The physical attraction was still very much there, the chemistry too, but they were in her territory now; their lives had irrevocably changed and different rules applied. Not just that, but she was grieving about the accident, stressing about her father, worrying about Dom. Getting tangled up in all of that would just complicate everything, for them both.

He imagined her father riding proudly through these woods and knew he couldn't promise her anything about his recovery and certainly wasn't going to lie just to make her feel better. Hell, they'd just agreed to always be honest. He tipped her chin so he could look into her eyes, wanting to kiss her again but knowing that was over now. 'I hope he will. In time.'

'And we both know he may not have enough time, *sì*? I… I need to get back to the palace, Lucas. There may be more news.' Her eyes closed

briefly and he could see her mentally putting the kiss into a box and closing the lid, but not before the heat hit her cheeks too. 'Is it okay if we meet in the morning at breakfast? I'll ask Paulo to set it up in the Lega room at eight.'

'Absolutely. About before…' He ran his thumb across her swollen lips, leaving her in no doubt he was referring to the kiss. 'We shouldn't have—'

'I know. I know. We got carried away. There's so much going on. Too much. Forget it happened. Please.'

He nodded, unable to agree out loud. He would try, of course. But forgetting a blazing, desperate kiss like that wasn't going to happen any time soon.

If ever.

CHAPTER SIX

She didn't sleep, of course. Not for the next three days.

How could she when there was so much to think about? Her father. Domenico. The baby… Oh, she couldn't stop thinking about that as it grew inside her.

And Lucas.

Here he was, strolling down the main staircase as if he was meant to be here. Her heart rate doubled at the sight of him. He was dressed in smart-casual beige chinos and a collared pale blue polo shirt that hugged his swim-assisted muscles, freshly shaved and with a smattering of grey in his hair that she hadn't noticed before. But, then, she'd been too transfixed by his eyes and his kisses and trying to work out how they could move forward.

He'd been here three days and she'd been the perfect hostess, showing him around her country, taking him on walks through the gardens, even a trip to the theatre to see a Christmas play. They were the epitome of polite and reserved, not referring again to the kiss, but they also hadn't got anything sorted out about the baby…neither of them seemed to have the stomach to start discussing a future that was months away.

So they'd fallen into a semi-domestic routine of meeting for breakfast, making small talk, reading through social media comments.

It was killing her.

Being so close every day and not being able to touch him.

She pretended she was fine. He kept his distance. He didn't touch her. In fact, it was almost as if he went out of his way not to touch her, as if he'd switched off that part of him. But she couldn't find her off switch. And her body strained for just the brush of his hand against hers.

Three days and her sexual awareness was off the scale. But at least he'd stayed.

He nodded as he reached the bottom stair. No air kisses. Still no kiss at all. 'Good morning, Giada.'

'Hello, Lucas.'

He'd called her Gigi down at the lake that first evening here, she remembered, and then realised she was looking at him for a sign. Something, anything to let her know what was going on in his head. Was he reliving that kiss the way she did night after night? Was he mentally pushing her up against a tree?

His face was a mask of politeness and she knew he'd retreated back behind the barrier he was too fond of constructing to keep himself free from emotional entanglements. Was that because of the way his family had treated him?

And why did it matter so much to her? She just couldn't fathom how he'd worked his way under her skin, into her head.

He nodded at her arm. 'Any better today? I see you've mastered the art of the sling.'

'The throbbing's stopped and the swelling's getting better.' She raised her right arm. 'Maria did the sling. We watched a video on the internet. She's determined to get it right for…when you're not here.'

Because there would be a time, she knew, when he would have to go back to his work. Of course, his life was there while hers was here—for the foreseeable future if not for ever, and especially while her father was sick.

There was no way she could do what Dom had done and give any of this up. She had responsibilities and duties to perform for her nation and her family. But maybe Lucas could move here? Maybe they could try to be a family? It could happen. If they both wanted it.

Stupid idea.

He was going to leave and she was going to stay. She would do the lioness's share of the child-care and he would, no doubt, appear when he saw fit. She'd cope. She had more than enough help. Everything would be fine.

'I see.' His jaw twitched and then tightened but he didn't say anything else.

In many ways he was right to put up barriers. The future was too unsure and adding her heart into the mix wasn't going to help any of them. Just one touch from him and she was all but un-done but they had very different paths to follow, tied only by their child…and she knew how dis-tant a father could be even if he was in the same room, so she couldn't let her feelings for this man get any stronger. 'Let's get something to eat.'

'I do like this room. It's so unlike everywhere else in the palace,' he said as he walked into the cosy yellow breakfast room with its simple six-seater table and a huge picture window that overlooked the kitchen gardens. She'd originally chosen this room because she'd thought he'd feel more relaxed here—she always did. 'When we first came in here I thought we'd be twenty feet apart, one each end of a long table.'

It appeared they were doing small-talk today. 'It's one of my favourite rooms in the whole pal-ace, probably because it isn't so staid or formal. Domenico and I ate breakfast in here for years

before heading off to school.' She ran her fingers over the dented mahogany and smiled at the memories of her mother shushing them as they'd chattered and laughed together. Of looking up to her clever, handsome brother and not minding one bit about how he'd refuse to speak to her in front of his friends, because in private he'd tickle her and, just to stop her bothering him, had even let her put nail varnish on his toes…as long as he could wipe it off before school the next day. Life had been so much simpler for them all back then. 'I doubt he even eats breakfast these days.'

'Probably shovels in a protein bar on the way to work, like I do.' Lucas picked up a plate and sniffed the air. 'Smells great. I'm starving.'

At least one of them had an appetite then. Lack of sleep made her head hurt and her tummy roil.

She prompted him to help himself from the silver platters on the side table that held bacon, eggs, pancakes and fruit.

He piled a stack of pancakes onto his plate alongside bacon and blueberries. 'Have you heard any more news about your father?'

'Dom texted to say Papa was still stable. Nothing new. That's good, right? I mean…obviously it would be better if he was out of the coma.'

'They're keeping him in the coma to give his brain time to heal from the surgery,' he said in the kind of tone you'd use to a young child.

'I understand that, but I want to fast-forward to where he wakes up. But then we'll have to tell him about this…' She put her hand over her belly, convinced she was bigger now than yesterday, although that was likely improbable. Lucas's eyes drifted to her stomach and she could see the softening there, the undisguised interest. 'Soon enough I'll be too big to hide the fact I'm pregnant.'

He stared at her then. 'Is everything okay?'

'As far as I know. Is it stupid to want to have a scan every day just to watch the baby growing?'

He shook his head. 'Not at all. Every mother wants reassurance.'

And father too? 'Oh, I never sent you the ultrasound video. Here.' She sat at the table and opened her digital tablet, scrolled through and clicked. The *whoosh-um-whoosh-um-whoosh-um* echoed around the room. 'Shoot! Better turn the volume off in case anyone comes in.'

He sat down opposite her and shook his head, quite vehemently. 'Just email it to me. I can look later.'

His attitude stung. 'What's wrong?'

'Nothing.'

She'd had enough of this tiptoeing around; they'd been doing that for three days and it was only making things worse. 'Is it the kiss? Are

you still angry about it? Or is it something else? The baby?'

'Angry?' He frowned at her words then his shoulders dropped and he exhaled heavily. 'No, Giada, not at you. But I am…frustrated that we got into this situation.'

'You have to admit it was fun, though.' She shrugged, trying to make a joke. She wanted to see him smile, for reassurance more than anything but also because he looked so good when he let his guard down. 'I think you're still sore about that kiss.'

He flinched at the memory. 'I'm just glad we pressed the stop button.'

Funny, she hadn't been thinking that at all—sure, in theory, he was right, but it hadn't stopped her wanting a rerun. 'There's a lot for us to deal with at the moment. We can't help it if emotions run high and we get…um…carried away.'

'We *can* help it.' He gaped at her. 'We can't just let our emotions run amok and do what we want. You know full well anyone could have seen us and spread gossip and you certainly don't want to have to deal with that.'

'You sound just like my father.'

'That's probably the age difference showing itself.' He speared a piece of pancake with his fork.

'Ouch, Lucas. You didn't think much about that down by the lake. Or three months ago. Not when

you had your hands on me.' She put her palm near her breast where his mouth had been. Where she wanted it again. And his eyes followed, his pupils widening.

He rubbed his forehead with his fingers. 'Giada, please. This is very difficult.'

'I know and you're not helping. I'm trying to get my head around things and a bit of light relief will keep me sane. It would be great if you could loosen up a bit.'

He put down his knife and fork. 'This is who I am, Giada. I'm a doctor, not a clown.'

'You did a lot more smiling back in August.'

'Things were very different then.'

'You don't say.' She'd been able to cajole him then, seduce him. He'd been a challenge and she'd managed to push through his reserve. She'd had a glimpse of the real Lucas Beaufort, unfettered, unworried, unconstrained, but she didn't know if she had the strength or emotional wherewithal to do it again with everything else going on.

She managed a mouthful of coffee then remembered it made her queasy. Or maybe it was the realisation that he'd retreated so far he wasn't planning on coming back any time soon that made her tummy hurt. Oh, he was a challenge all right. 'Right, eat up your breakfast and then we can get on with the day.'

She put her digital tablet back onto the table and turned it on but he covered it with his palm.

'Do you want to go through the media comments?'

'Too late. I've already looked. Through my fingers, before I got up.'

He glared at her. 'Why?'

'What can I say? I'm an independent woman. I was awake half the night and it seemed like a good use of my time.' Instead of Lucas bearing witness to some of the less savoury comments about her. *Princess Party… The Giada Problem…*

Shaking his head, irritated, he leaned forward and frowned. Again. 'What did they say?'

'There are still a lot of good wishes. Many, many from all around the world. But there are questions too. Why the silence now? Three days and no more updates. Where is Domenico? Where is the King? When is he being brought back to Isola Verde?'

He nodded curtly. 'All questions that can either be ignored or pacified with non-specific statements.'

'I'm not good at being impartial and non-specific when it's about my family.'

He shrugged. 'As a doctor you learn to keep your emotions to yourself. It isn't helpful or professional to get upset in front of a patient. I can do noncommittal when necessary.'

'Yes, Captain Sensible. I'd say you've achieved expert level.'

He blinked and sat up straight as he took in her words. Maybe no one had ever spoken so forthrightly to him before? He seemed to think it through and then wrestle inwardly for a couple of moments before he answered her. 'Tomorrow I will check them first. It's not good to look at that before you even get out of bed.'

'Okay. It's a date.' She dug for a smile, trying to show him that his attitude towards her would not bring her down. 'And today I have a treat in store for you.'

'Oh?' His expression was wary.

'Don't worry, I'm not going to lose control and kiss you again.' She watched the sudden flare of heat in his eyes and smiled to herself. Oh, yes. Lucas Beaufort could say what he liked, but no matter how much he tried he couldn't always mask the way his body reacted to her. 'We are going to see my hospital.'

He'd been too hard on her, he knew that, and guilt bit.

But it was a self-preservation thing. If he was going to survive this visit he needed to keep his distance from her. Even so, the need to see her smile again wound itself inside him. She wanted funny and relaxed but he was serious and uptight. It was yet another reason why they were so mismatched. And yet...there was something between them that went deeper, so deep it felt as if there was a real physical connection.

Indeed, the physicality was so intense it spooked him. How could it be that two people turned each other on so much and yet couldn't manage more than half a dozen civil words?

It was his fault. He was trying too hard to protect them both from the fallout of another ill-advised liaison. But should he try to loosen up? Could he be the man he'd been in August when she'd smashed his barriers down? When it had been about the now and not about the consequences?

Could he be the man she wanted him to be?

Or would that mean a personality transplant?

Thing was, he wanted to try, and that shook him more than anything else.

The car pulled up outside an impressive state-of-the-art glass-fronted building. Given everything that was happening, the new Isola Verde Hospital hadn't been at the forefront of his mind but he could feel her enthusiasm rising as they stepped inside and he felt a similar prickle of excitement.

Despite protestations, she'd told Maria to wait

in the car, saying, 'I'm fine. I don't need baby-sitting all the time.' Then she'd rolled her eyes at Lucas. 'It's suffocating to have someone in your face all the time.'

'A bodyguard is for your own safety, surely?'

'Please don't you start too. It's annoying. Papa likes an entourage, I prefer to go incognito.' She winked. 'Besides, no one's going to bother me with you by my side. One grumpy look and you'll scare them half to death.'

He didn't know what to say to that. Mainly because she was right. There was no middle ground between them; it was either all intense desire or polite and awkward. And that, he knew, was all on him.

As they walked in a young woman dashed from behind the reception desk and curtsied. 'Your Highness.' She added something else that Lucas didn't understand.

Giada smiled and replied in English. 'I am not here on an official visit. An escort from management isn't necessary, thank you. I'm just showing a doctor friend of mine around the hospital.'

'Yes, Your Highness. Have a good day.'

'We had the official opening a few weeks ago.' Giada turned back to Lucas, her high pony-tail swishing and heels clicking as they walked across the tiled floor. This was only a social visit but she was dressed smartly in a vivid blue silk blouse and curve-enhancing black pencil skirt that kicked out at the knees. And stiletto heels.

Man, those heels. The stuff men's dreams were made of. Yes, he may have been grumpy but a lot of that was due to sexual frustration. More than once he'd had to stop himself from touching her. Sure, he'd made up his mind that he would put a stop to any more kissing, but that didn't mean he *wanted* to put a stop to it. He was trying hard here…but…stilettoes.

The place looked like a hotel with comfortable sofas and friendly welcoming staff, only the fresh disinfectant smell and signs pointing the way to Emergency, Cardiac Care and specialist wards giving away the fact they were in a clinical environment. There was a tall Christmas tree right by the front door with piles of Christmas gifts underneath.

Giada smiled as she followed his gaze. 'I wanted to make it a place where people felt looked after rather than put off by a sterile cold atmosphere.'

'We try to achieve the same at Seattle General. The annual Christmas display is always eye-catching and the kids love it.' He felt a pang of homesickness then. How comforting it would be to slip back into his old routine of work, swim, work. Yeah, not much of a life, but it was steady and predictable. Unlike life with Giada so far.

'You look like you're missing your day job. I imagine being on this island is pretty boring.' She tugged on his arm. 'Come see the ER.'

They followed the sign towards the emergency department but Lucas was stopped in his tracks by a large portrait on the wall. A stunning woman with commanding brown eyes and long dark hair swept up into a loose bun, wearing a tiara, a formal gown of purple and silver and a beautiful smile looked down at him. Giada in all her regal glory. His heart stalled as he tried to read the plaque underneath, but it was in Isola Verdian. 'What does it say?'

Her cheeks turned pink as she cleared her throat and read out, '"Our nation thanks with all our hearts Giada, the People's Princess, for bestowing this wonderful facility for the benefit of everyone in Isola Verde."' She gave an embarrassed smile. 'I asked them not to put it up but they insisted.'

'The People's Princess? They obviously love you.'

'Some do. Some really don't. Well...' She held up her sling-free hand. 'That's not entirely true. I was popular as a child, but in my late teens and early twenties not so much. It hasn't always been easy. I disgraced myself more than a few times and I've worked hard on my reputation over the last couple of years.'

'This hospital is an amazing achievement.'

She huffed. 'I wanted to do something that will benefit everyone.'

'Your father must be very proud of you.'

Her throat made a funny noise—half laugh, half derision. 'You don't know Papa. As far as he's concerned, once trouble, always trouble. He was so used to hearing bad things about me he didn't trust the good stuff.'

'So why did you decide to do this instead of partying on yachts?'

She led him down the long corridor following signs to ER, her demeanour brisk. 'Let's just say I had a life lesson that made me realise that my legacy shouldn't be about the trouble I caused but about the good I could do.'

'Sounds serious. What happened?'

She shook her head and cast her gaze around, suddenly guarded and serious. 'Long story. Not for here. You don't need to know. No one does.'

'Will I need to do an internet search on it? Will our child uncover things I don't know about you? What happened to being honest?' He wasn't sure how far to push it. He was out of his depth when it came to relationships and trust.

Her eyes closed for a second. 'I'm not proud of my silly past. But, no, I hope we managed to keep that particular escapade under wraps.'

He was intrigued. 'Tell me—'

'Hey!'

They were interrupted by a young man of about twenty pushing past them, shouting something in Isola Verdian. 'What's he saying?'

Giada froze, concerned. 'He's saying, "Help. Help my friend."'

Lucas went into autopilot, his focus narrowing in on the guy and already going through a mental checklist of possible scenarios, but assuming nothing. 'Ask him where. Where is his friend?'

Giada blinked and spoke to the man, who was white and jittery with panic, and then followed his pointed finger behind them. 'There. Whoa.' She grabbed Lucas's arm tightly. *'Oddio.'*

Lucas whirled round and saw a side entrance he hadn't noticed before, the door rattling in the wind. On the ground, curled in a foetal position, was another man. Judging by the thick trail of red behind him, he looked as if he was bleeding out.

Okay.

Running to the man, Lucas shouted over his shoulder, 'Gigi, go to the ER and get help.'

'What?' Instead of continuing along the corridor, she followed Lucas, her eyes wide and scared as she too bent and stared at the man on the floor as if she couldn't drag her eyes away.

'Don't look. Look at me.' She may have built the hospital but she wasn't used to seeing the things he had. Straightening, he took her by the shoulders and made her focus on him. 'Gigi, I need you do something for me.'

'Wh-what?'

'Go to the ER. Quickly. Get help.'

'Okay.' She nodded, and looked as if she was mentally shaking herself, but she didn't move. 'ER. Yes.'

'Are there panic buttons here? Code buttons anywhere on these walls?' He scanned the walls but there were no tell-tale red buttons anywhere. In other hospitals they had them at strategic points for staff members to get help in an emergency.

'I… I don't know.'

'The ER, Giada.' He inhaled and blew out, biting back the retort that she'd insisted on leaving Maria at the car. 'I don't have a pager to send a code to the trauma team and I can't leave him. You have to go. Now, Giada.'

'*Sì.*'

He pushed away his emotions and focused back on the emergency at hand. He couldn't get to grips with how to act with Giada, had no idea how to be a decent father, how to fit into this Royal family, was making a bad fist at being a friend. But this? This he could do.

He knelt on the floor, doing a quick visual assessment of their patient. Losing consciousness. Pale. Glasgow Coma Scale… He was trying to work it out, and hoped the team here used the same terminology as he did. 'Hey, what happened? *Damn.* I don't speak your language. Doctor.' Enunciating slowly, Lucas pointed to his chest. 'I'm a doctor.'

The teenager's eyes flickered open then closed again. The friend hovered just out of Lucas's peripheral vision.

Lucas turned his head. 'What happened? Tell me.'

'Parkour.'

'English?' Lucas demanded. 'Do you speak English?'

The man rotated his shaking hand from side to side. A little English. 'Parkour.'

Just as the man said it, Lucas peeled away his patient's hands and saw a railing spike had perforated his abdomen on the left side. He tried to prise the man's hands further away so he could see the entry point and try to stem the bleeding. The spike would need to be surgically removed to prevent further damage, although judging by the blood loss they'd be fighting an uphill battle.

The man's pulse was thin and thready and he was already sinking into unconsciousness. There was a lot of blood. And, probably, very little time to save him.

'Giada!' he called to her back as she hurried

away. 'Tell them to hurry. We need a trolley. Man-power. Fluids. Large-bore IVs. Resus.'

'Okay. Got it.' She nodded again and disappeared around the corner.

'Hey, buddy. Hey.' Lowering his face to the man, Lucas checked for breathing.

Nothing.

Cursing at being knee-deep in blood with no equipment, he laid the man flat, preparing for CPR. 'Okay. You're not going to die on my watch.'

He needed to somehow stop blood loss and do chest compressions at the same time. He could jump from one to the other and it could be manageable on his own, but not realistic for long. The friend was sitting on the floor now, head in his hands, incapable of anything but sobbing into his knees. 'Hey. Friend! Come here.'

The man didn't even raise his head, just shook it.

Not good enough. Lucas knew he was scared, but this was literally a life and death situation. 'I. Need. You. *Please.*'

But no dice. Lucas clenched his jaw. It wasn't the first time he'd had to improvise. He crawled to his patient's side and placed his hands over the man's ribcage.

And then, just as he thought he was going to have to go solo on this, he heard the rattle of a gurney, raised voices and fast footsteps. In a break between compressions he glanced over and there was Giada, running in those damned high heels, leading a team with trolleys and equipment.

His belly did a sudden leap. He didn't think he'd ever been so pleased to see her.

But he wasn't sure it was because she'd brought the cavalry.

CHAPTER SEVEN

ONCE SHE'D SETTLED the frightened friend with a nursing assistant and a hot drink, Giada sidled back to the corridor to watch Lucas in action. Truth was, she couldn't take her eyes off him. He commanded the space and the staff who had come running, stopped and listened and then did as he asked.

He was gentle yet affirmative. Completely in control and yet listening to input. Decisive and yet compassionate and totally in his element.

How could she even entertain the thought he might want to come and live in the palace and play at being consort when he could work miracles like this? The man was more at home elbow deep in blood than with Da Vinci paintings and public receptions.

He directed the CPR effort. He took control of the count to lift the man onto the gurney. He slid the IV bore into a vein. He did something to help the man breathe—a tube into his throat she thought she saw—and attached him to a portable oxygen tube. He gave the briefest satisfied nod when they got a trace on the ECG.

He sent someone to get a portable X-ray, asked another to arrange a CT scan, then told yet another to page the general surgeons as they all filed into the ER department with the trolley and the equipment and a sense of being in total control. The last thing she saw as the resuscitation room door swung closed was his gaze on her. Just for a moment.

Even from here she could see the buzz in his eyes.

And something else…something that simmered when his guard was down. Something that made her hot all over. Power, control, authority, command. He was in his element and it suited him. Very much.

Then she was locked out of the room and quite right too. No one needed a silly princess messing things up in there.

And, unfortunately, everyone was very aware that she was here. She had to make polite small talk with the staff and the patients and pretend she hadn't just seen a man almost die. The hospital chief had heard she was here and came to talk to her about budgets. There was an invitation to a hospital bed push charity event in the new year. Then the one thing she'd been avoiding…a question about her father.

'He's…he's stable.' She reiterated the words her brother told her every day, twice a day, when they spoke.

'Bring him home, Your Highness,' one of the senior nurses said as Giada sat down at the nurses' station and waited for Lucas to be finished. 'We'll look after him here. Where is he?'

'In very good hands.' With his son. The future King. Across the world. Her heart twisted and she suddenly understood how it felt to be her brother, torn between duty and wanting to be somewhere else entirely.

'That is good.' The nurse exhaled. 'I am praying for him. For you all.'

'Thank you, Bianca.'

After dropping a curtsey, the nurse's eyes flicked over Giada's body and she could have sworn Bianca's gaze stopped at her breasts and then went down to her belly. 'And can I say how well you look, Your Highness.'

Oh.

Was her pregnancy so obvious? Was she showing? Giada's cheeks burned and she fisted her hands to stop herself running them across her abdomen. Smiling as sweetly as she could, she nodded to Bianca. 'Isola Verde always makes me feel better.'

She heard laughter and was grateful for the distraction, but when she turned to see where it was coming from she was surprised to see Lucas, his head tipped back, laughing at something Alberto, the head of ER, had said. *Laughing?*

She watched as the two men chatted. Alberto did an action as if he was kicking a ball, then his eyes widened and he hid his head in his hands… Missing a goal? She didn't know. Sport didn't interest her. Lucas shook his head and raised his hands at Alberto, then laughed again.

She was surprised to feel a jab of hurt. Was Lucas only a stuffed shirt with her? She noticed he'd changed into the hospital scrubs, a bag saying 'Hospital Property' in his hand, which no doubt contained his stained clothes.

At the palace, in her territory, he was out of his comfort zone and probably felt as if he needed to be polite and formal. With the baby business he was reserved and trying to do the right thing. As was she. All of which amounted to stiff conversation and frustration, because they were both trying to be things they were not.

But she'd helped him relax before… And she was going to do it again.

Yes. She decided at that moment she would find the Lucas she'd fallen for.

Wait. Fallen for?

Didn't she mean fallen pregnant with?

Yes. That was what she'd meant.

He shook hands with Alberto then made his

way over to her. 'Hello, I didn't realise you'd waited for me.'

'I didn't know how long you'd be, so I thought I'd hang around. As it is, I managed to see a couple of the managers and we arranged some meetings.' She stood up. 'You look relaxed. I'm assuming everything's okay?'

'Yes, and you were great, thank you, Gigi. Um…' His eyes flickered to the nurses who were watching them and he corrected himself. 'I mean Your Highness.'

'Gigi is more than fine. How is he?'

Lucas gently took her elbow and walked her towards the ER department exit. 'He's gone to Theatre. He's actually very lucky, apart from the huge blood loss which would have killed him. The spike missed most of his internal organs. We'll have to remove his spleen and possibly fix a laceration to his kidney, but he's going to recover well.'

She looked up at him, glad he was holding her arm, glad he was steady and capable and not like the friend who hadn't been able to cope. Not like her, who had been initially too shocked to move. 'You were magnificent, Lucas.'

He raised a shoulder. 'Just doing what I've been trained to do.'

'You do it well. You're buzzing. Glowing.'

He looked thoughtful for a minute and stretched

his fingers out in front of him, his eyes glittering. 'I guess I am…er, buzzy. You get such an adrenalin hit and it takes a while to wear off. I thought I'd got used to it, but here…it's a new environment. I didn't speak the language or know the staff, but we still saved him.'

'*You* did.'

'It was very definitely a group effort.' He seemed so relaxed and freed up now. It had been a genius idea to bring him here, to this familiar environment.

They made their way to the front desk and out into the glare of the early afternoon sun. He stopped and turned to her. 'You once said to me it feels good to do good, and you're right.'

'I said that?' She laughed, putting her hand to her heart. 'I am so profound.'

'Sometimes you really are surprising, Gigi.' He smiled then and she loved the way his face relaxed, his whole body leaning into her.

She couldn't help but lean into him, too. Just the simple act of his hand on her arm strengthened the connection. But she ached for more. For him to touch her face, to run her hair though his fingers, to slide his mouth over hers.

But he wasn't going to, not here anyway.

And *Gigi*. It came naturally to him now. Such a small step, but he wasn't putting up that barrier quite as high as he had been. When he laughed, when he was relaxed, when he looked at her with glittering eyes her whole body leaned towards him, wanting more, wanting him. 'You had everyone doing what you told them to do.'

He shrugged again. 'I hope I didn't step on anyone's toes.'

'Not at all. I explained who you are and told them to let you do your stuff.'

'Even so, I wouldn't like someone coming into my department and telling me what to do.'

They reached their car, which was idling in the visitors' car park out front. She paused and wondered how he was going to take her next comment. 'They were grateful. In fact, they asked if you could stay on for a few hours.'

He turned to look back at the hospital, eyes wistful. 'To work? Here? Now?'

'They're short-staffed and, yes, I know they are in Seattle too. But you're here and it would do more good. And you'd get to feel even better.' She bit her lip. 'I said yes.'

'Without discussing it with me?' But he didn't look angry, he looked energised. 'Without paperwork? I'm not registered to work in this country.'

'I have fast-tracked the paperwork with the hospital administrator. The last few days have been boring and frustrating for you, I know. I can't entertain you all the time. I'm needed at the palace for briefings and meetings.'

'I don't need to be entertained, Giada.' His eyebrows rose in mock offence but he didn't say it was the most stupid idea she'd ever had.

'Seeing as you won't engage in the kind of entertaining that will soothe both mind and body, you might as well get out from under my feet.'

Luckily, he understood what she was trying to say. 'Wait.' He glanced around, checking to see if anyone was listening. 'You're telling me to go to work so we don't…'

'Get carried away,' she whispered, doing air quotes over her words. 'Like at the lake. Like in August. It's a good plan, *si*? When we're together we either argue or can't keep our hands off each other. There's no middle ground. And I can't spend all day, every day with you either arguing or dying of sexual frustration. Personally, I think you're grumpy because you don't have enough sex.' She held up her hand at his attempts to stop her speaking. 'Your mind is too active and your body is too pent up with excess energy, or too much buzz from saving all those lives. Sex would relieve all of that and make you feel even better. Imagine that. Remember how good it felt?'

A corner of his mouth twitched and the glittering in his eyes intensified. Oh, yes, he remembered. But he shook his head. 'I never read about that remedy in any science journal. Who's the doctor here?'

'I know, I know. But I'm right? *Si?* And, seeing as you don't think sex with me is a good idea, we need to have another plan.'

'Gigi…' He looked as if he would either devour her right now or explode with frustration.

'Unless you *do* think sex with me is a good idea?'

He couldn't lie. His eyes told her that he thought sex would be a very good idea. But he growled, 'This isn't helping. I'm trying to do the right thing.'

'Avoiding the subject won't make it go away, so maybe we should face it head on. For the record, I think sex with you would be fantastic. I'm just not sure about what happens after that.'

He frowned. 'That's exactly the problem.'

'It's not a problem.' She leaned closer, close enough for her to breathe in his freshly showered scent, close enough to look deep into his eyes, but not so close as to arouse suspicions from any onlookers. 'A conundrum, maybe. A puzzle.' She put her hand on his chest and gave a very gentle push. 'Now…go back to work.'

'Are you sure?' Just one glance at his eyes told her she had him. He was interested and he wasn't hiding it. 'You don't need me?'

'No. Go do your thing. I don't need you this afternoon.'

Funny thing was, she almost did, as much as

she'd needed anyone. She liked his logical thinking. He *listened* to her and that was something new in her life when it came to the people close to her. Usually, she was told she was too young, too inexperienced or just a distraction. Or someone who could be used as a stepping stone to the monarchy's inner circle and influencers. Someone to trample all over her. But Lucas was different; he didn't want to use her. 'The minute you saw that kid your whole demeanour changed. You were born to be a doctor, Lucas, anyone could see that. I could never get in the way of you doing what you're called to do. Just…'

'Just what?'

'I'd like to see you after work and hear all about it.' She waved her hand to dismiss him, as if she didn't need him or want him, when every cell in her body strained for him. She took the paper bag from his hand. 'Now, get back to work. I'll get your clothes laundered and bring some fresh ones. I'm going to make a reservation for dinner. I'll be here at six o'clock.'

CHAPTER EIGHT

HE WAS LATE, of course, as doctors generally were, and she clearly wasn't used to being kept waiting. 'What happened to six o'clock, Lucas?' she half joked, when he arrived breathless from running the length of the ER corridor. But he could see she was irritated.

He looked at his watch and grimaced. Never a good look to keep a woman waiting, particularly not a princess. 'Twenty-three minutes late. I am so sorry. But I just couldn't leave halfway through stabilising an airway for a four-year-old girl.'

She looked horrified. 'Oh! No, of course not. What happened to her?'

'Fell off her pony. Neck injury. Too traumatised to keep still for a scan so we had to sedate her.'

'And...?'

'She's going to be sore for a few weeks, but no broken bones and no long-term damage.'

Gigi brightened, fist pumping her slingless left hand. In fact, when he looked, both wrists were sling-free and all she had on now was a bandage on her damaged arm. 'Thank goodness. So you had the parkour incident, a pony incident, what else did you do?'

He wasn't used to going over his day with anyone and he had to admit it was kind of cool to be able to debrief with someone who was actually interested. He climbed into the car and sat next to her in the back, also unused to being chauffeured. But at least here they could talk. 'One difficult shoulder dislocation. Two acute cardiac arrests. A couple of twisted ankles—'

'And a partridge in a pear tree?' She laughed, looking almost as energised as he felt by his work. 'Sounds busy. And the staff were nice to you?'

'Of course. The language is a problem, although most of the staff seem to speak some English, the patients too. At first we did a lot of gesturing and speaking very slowly, and then I found an app that translates from English into Isola Verdian, which made things a lot easier.' He brandished his phone and showed her the app. 'I speak and it translates. Clever. So we managed. We didn't have the chance not to, to be honest. There's never a quiet day in ER, but that's why I love it.'

'I can see that.'

'We did have one sad case…an elderly lady with dementia. The daughter found her on the floor at home. It's clear she needs to be in care, but she's resisting. The daughter feels guilty about not being able to cope and is angry at her brother for not helping enough, even though they're meant to split the care equally. The son wishes it would all disappear so he can get on with his life. Neither of them agreed on anything.'

Their bickering had made him realise how easy it could be to slide into selfishness and not put the most important person as a priority. As he'd watched, he'd decided he'd prioritise his baby and would work on compromising with Giada, however difficult that would be.

She rolled her pretty eyes. 'Families, eh?'

He shrugged. 'Why is it always families that make your heart hurt?'

She looked at him then for a second, two. 'I don't know, Lucas.'

Damn. He'd obviously reminded her of her own family troubles and he regretted mentioning anything, especially as they were finally getting along. For a few moments she'd been the woman from August and now he'd brought her very definitely back to being the haunted November Giada. 'How was your day?'

She sighed. 'I'm trying to get up to speed with the succession plan, just in case...well, you know, just in case Domenico becomes King soon. There are protocols we need to put in place the minute any announcement is made.'

'It may not get to that for a very long time.' Lucas smiled, trying to be positive.

But she shook her head, as sadness filled her eyes. 'Dom says he spends all his spare time at Papa's side, pretending to be a concerned friend rather than his son, just so no gossip gets out. There's no change. Dom talks to him, even though he's in a coma. Apparently, there's research that says the patient can hear even if they can't respond. At least, they are comforted by a familiar voice. I thought I might send some voice messages to the hospital for him. What do you think?'

'Great idea. Anything to help.'

'If you think it will? I'll do some when I get home.' Her stomach growled. 'Okay, I need food now. This baby is hungry and isn't wanting to wait.'

'What do you need? Pizza? Pasta? Indian?' He realised his whole body smiled in response to her nourishing his child. He was getting used to the thought of being a father, his heart making space for a daughter or a son.

Or both?

The idea of a growing family shook him. He didn't do families. And yet…

'I have the perfect place in mind.' Gigi opened the sliding hatch in the grille between the front and back seats and spoke to Maria. 'Angelo's, please.'

They drove for a few minutes through the back streets then wound down a secluded cobbled road that became narrower and narrower until they reached a small sandy cove. The only building there was a small seafront restaurant that looked more like someone's home. It had a white-painted stone facade with table and chairs outside, glorious cooking smells tinging the air, and a flat roof festooned with red flowers.

The owner greeted them as if they were long lost friends, and when Giada introduced them Lucas understood why. 'Angelo is the father of one of my closest school friends.'

There was no formal bow, just a bear hug from the chef, and it was easy to see that Angelo had a lot of affection for Gigi. The feeling was clearly mutual. 'He also makes the best risotto in the country.'

Lucas nipped into the restroom to change out of the scrubs and into the clothes she'd brought him—a collared shirt, jacket and chinos, then he was led upstairs to a roof garden that looked out to the Mediterranean. Lucas was surprised to see no other diners, no set tables apart from theirs. But Giada wasn't sitting, she was leaning against a railing and looking at the water, taking greedy deep breaths, her shoulders instantly relaxing.

He took a moment to just look at her in profile. Her lush dark hair cascaded over her shoulders, and he ached to thrust his hands into those curls and run them through the soft silkiness. From this position he could see the tiny swell of her belly and he wanted to press his hands there too, to feel the outlines of her growing body. She was stunning.

If only…

If only what? If only she wasn't a princess destined to be constrained by duty? If only there weren't so many complications?

As if she felt him looking she turned and smiled. 'There you are. More comfortable?'

He tried to find his voice but he was blown away by the sight of her silhouetted by the setting sun, and all his words were gone. So he just walked to her and settled against the railing, keeping his distance. Wishing he didn't have to.

She turned to him. 'We have the place to ourselves.'

'When you said you'd book, I didn't think you meant the whole restaurant.'

She nodded. 'All taken care of. Including the bill.'

Well, damn, she certainly wouldn't be depending on him for financial assistance for their baby—although he'd make sure she got it.

He looked out to the orange-red horizon, across

syrupy blue water dotted with the occasional yacht or fishing boat. 'The view is amazing.'

'You can see the palace from almost everywhere on the island, apart from here. Here, I forget who I am supposed to be and get to be just Gigi.' Inhaling deeply, she pointed out to the right, towards a little wooded area accessed by a rickety metal gate that he could just about pick out in the dusk. 'Just beyond that gate is Angelo's private beach. When I was younger I used to sneak out to meet my friends there, until I got caught by one of the security team as I was racing through the palace gardens with a bottle of wine I'd stolen from the palace cellars. I got my marching orders from Papa and was grounded for a month. Being grounded as a princess means guards at your door...trust me, it's not fun.'

He smiled at the thought. 'I hope our baby is less trouble than you or I'm going to go prematurely grey.'

'Oops. Too late.' She reached out to the little silver strands at the side of his head and gave a little shrug, mock pity on her face.

He touched her hand, cupping her fingers in his. 'Hey! I've only had these greys for four days.'

'You're saying I've turned you into a silver fox in just four days?' She laughed. 'I don't believe you.'

'Okay, maybe they appeared a few months ago.

Since… August?' The idea she'd turned his hair silver was ridiculous and yet…he had felt tangled up since August. But he laughed and it felt freeing, as if something inside him was unravelling.

'Really? These are all my fault?' She shook her head but kept looking at him with a curious expression. 'You look so good when you smile, Lucas. Even better when you laugh. You seem different tonight.'

'Today was a good day. I was useful, I saved some lives, made some friends.' He leaned back against the railing, simply because the view of her was far better than anything nature had created.

Her hand slid down his chest, taking his with it, and he thought about letting go but she held it tightly and he wondered if she needed to be held or comforted and he wasn't going to deny her that. She'd pushed him today and encouraged him to do the one thing that made him who he was: work. She'd recognised he'd needed that and he recognised she needed something too. He just wasn't sure he could give her it.

So they stood there, holding hands, chatting as if this were the most natural thing in the world. And his chest felt as if a golden light had sparked to life there. Truth was, she brought out a better side of him. Although she also brought out an extraordinary sexual need in him too.

'So, I have decided to *try* to lighten up a little

and make the most of being in Isola Verde,' he confessed. 'You're right... I am grumpy. I was thrown by our news. Thrown by being here and I retreated into myself.'

'Ah.' Her eyebrows rose. 'You don't like change much?'

'I've never really thought about it. I don't suppose I do, not in my private life at least. I guess that means I've grown insular.' He shook his head. 'And it seems that the more time I spend with you, the more I learn about myself.'

'Well, I am profound, after all.' She winked at him, teasing, finally slipping her hand out of his. 'You know what? I like it that we talk about important things, even if we do get a little heated.'

By heated she definitely didn't mean angry. Her eyes met his and lingered, simmering with something that reached into his gut and tugged. She bit her bottom lip and all his resolve to be friendly and open came crashing down around him. There were ramifications to them being less guarded. The most important one was letting flirting slip in, and who knew where that would lead?

But no matter how much he tried to hold his emotional barriers in place, they crumbled when she was around and he found himself wanting to relax and not fight any more. He wasn't used to sharing his thoughts and his feelings but it looked like he was going to have to try. 'I'm always telling my patients how important communication is and yet I need to work on it too. Clearly.'

'We all do. Including me…' Gigi paused while Angelo brought them antipasti. 'He doesn't have a menu, just cooks whatever's in season. It is always delicious.'

And, my God, it was. A selection of locally made cheeses and salami. Bread that was crisp and warm from the oven. Olives grown and cured less than a hundred yards away. Wine from the vineyard down the road. Then melt-in-the-mouth risotto. Lucas had two helpings and so did Gigi. It was good to see her feeding her body with the best that nature could provide. Good to see her laugh at the lighter moments of his tales of the ER and be interested in the drama of his day.

After dinner she took him down to the water's edge and they walked along the beach, which was lit by the silvery moon and huge flaming torches Alberto had driven into the sand. Lucas lingered behind her for a moment and watched as she navigated the sand in her wedges, and, much as it pained him to do so because her legs looked stunning in them, he called to her, 'Take them off.'

She whirled round, her eyes widening with interest. 'What did you say?'

'Take your shoes off.'

'Oh. Shoes. Right. Yes.' She shook her head as if she'd been thinking of something else entirely.

He nodded. 'Come paddle with me. It's the best remedy after a hard day's work.'

'Not skinny dipping this time? Oh, come on, don't look so sour, Lucas, you can't pretend it didn't happen.' Reaching with her good hand to slip off her sandal, she lost her balance and cried out, gripping his arm and laughing. 'If I fall it'll be all your fault, Dr Beaufort.'

But he was there, catching her, holding her, lowering her to the sand. He slipped her shoes off and they put their feet in the cool water, watching as it lapped lazily at their ankles. She was right, it had all happened and keeping a stiff upper lip about it wouldn't change a thing. He needed to loosen up.

'Is it okay if I…?' She leaned her head on his shoulder. 'Can I ask you a question?'

His heart hammered as he realised he preferred the joky kind of loosening up to the answering questions kind. 'Depends what it is.'

'Why me, Lucas? You could have any woman you want—yes, you could.' She laughed as he shook his head. 'Why me? Was it just because I was there? Was I…convenient?'

'God, no.' He hadn't been sure what she was going to ask, but he sure as hell hadn't imagined this. He thought back to that weekend. First impressions. The way she'd insinuated herself under his skin. And he tried to be honest…even though he'd never said anything like this before to any woman. Mainly because he'd never thought or felt anything like this before. 'You dazzled me, Gigi. You were so fresh and vibrant and happy and fun. Everything I'm not. And that bikini… wow. You're seriously beautiful. The question you should really be asking is why did you choose me? The serious, dependable, boring older man?'

He felt her shiver against him. 'Your kisses are far from boring, Lucas. You are amazing. Gorgeous, dedicated, handsome. Your passion for your job shows the minute you walk into the hospital and lasts a long time after you've left. You're older, sure, and that has a definite appeal—I am so over men my age. You just can't trust them.'

'What does that mean? I'm pretty sure I've always been the same me.'

'I imagine you have, but some guys need to grow the hell up.'

'What happened?' His interest was piqued.

She shook head. 'I want to talk about you, Lucas. That's far more interesting. When we met you were very aloof and out of reach, which, let me say, is also very sexy. At first, I admit, I thought you were a challenge. I wanted to know if I could…well, I wanted to seduce you.' She lifted her head and turned to look at him. 'God,

I sound so childish…but you turned me on the moment our eyes met.'

'And was I so easy to seduce?' He laughed as he drank in her beautiful features, her heated eyes, that perfect kissable mouth. Wanting to stay in this moment with her, he pushed back the cryptic comment that had accompanied the sudden hardness in her eyes as she'd talked about immature men. Something had happened and he was going to find out…later.

Right now, Lucas wanted to remember the seduction of that August weekend. 'I tried to do the right thing.'

'You put up a *bit* of a fight, sure.' She smiled, her eyes glittering.

He wanted a rerun of that weekend. No…he wanted this Gigi, the one who was carrying his child who could be sincere and focused and yet light-hearted. Who took her responsibilities seriously and yet saw the fun in everything. He wanted to make love to her here on the sand, in his bed back in Seattle, even in his gilt-edged suite at the palace. He wanted her.

She swallowed as she looked at him and he knew she was feeling the same tumult of emotions. This was getting deeper, their connection getting tighter, more complex. 'Oh, Lucas, I liked your loyalty to your friend, that you had standards. I liked it that you liked me too, but thought you shouldn't. That kind of…oh, chivalry, I guess, is lacking these days and is very sexy.'

His eyes roamed her face, dipping to her mouth. He could still taste her. Wanted to again. 'And now?'

She smiled. 'Nothing's changed. I still think you're sexy, but also deep and thoughtful. I know you can laugh and play, but you keep forgetting how. I think it's my job to help you remember.'

'Oh?'

She nodded, her hand creeping to his chest. 'And did I mention sexy? We could… You could kiss me again.'

He ran his thumb over her bottom lip, wishing, wanting to put his mouth there. 'You know I want to. But, like I said, you dazzle me. You make me want things I can't have.'

'You can have me.' Her eyes glittered again and she smiled, whispering the last word against his throat. 'Tonight.'

He inhaled her scent. Curled towards her throat. Imagined stripping off that dress. There was nothing he'd rather do. Nothing. So saying what he said next was damned hard. 'But that will cloud our judgement. Make decisions more difficult. If we're going to get through this with any sanity we have to just stay friends. Like today…we've got on well. We've talked; I feel as if we're making progress building a foundation for the future and for our child. We're having a good evening…at least I am.'

'We can make it even better.'

'Or a lot worse. Do you think we will be able to work things out when we're clouded by our emotions? Do you think we'll be able to decide what's best for our child when we're kissing each other senseless? And what next? We both know a relationship is unlikely. We can't go on chasing each other halfway around the world just for sex. What about when one of us decides they want to have a proper relationship with someone…more suitable?'

By that he meant she was destined to marry someone royal. Not a doctor. Not him. One day she'd tire of her sensible plaything and get real with someone out of his league, and then where would he stand?

And how would his heart recover? Because he knew…he knew that, to him, this was much more than desire. He liked her, admired her, enjoyed her. Wanted to spend more and more time with her, and that could only be to the detriment of both their futures.

'More suitable than a…stupid, silly princess, you mean? I thought you were different, Lucas, but it turns out that you're just like everyone else,' she ground out, as the tease whooshed out of her.

Then she pressed her lips together and he

watched her shrug on the metaphorical royal armour, straighten her back, her eyes glazing with an emotionless film, visibly retreating behind decorum. An eerie *sangfroid* she'd been taught to wear her whole life, to cover up any emotional reactions in public.

He'd expected her to shout at him, even wanted her to, but she was so quiet, so contained, so in control that it scared him. And he'd made her like that by his safeguarding and sensible choices. Yeah, he was the stupid one, not her. Never Gigi.

How to wind the clock back? 'Giada, I—'

'No.'

It was too late. He knew he'd pushed her away one time too many.

She scrambled up, grabbed her sandals and walked up the beach, waving goodbye and blowing kisses to Angelo, pretending everything was just fine. When in reality Lucas had just made everything a million times worse.

CHAPTER NINE

'GIADA, WAIT. WAIT!'

No.

She did not, would not wait for him. This was the last straw. She wasn't going to allow this to happen again. She was going to close herself up, instead of being an open book. She should have learnt that lesson with Leandro. Thought she had. Where were her promises not to get involved again? What happened to her resolve to keep every man at an emotional arm's length? To play and not let her heart get embroiled? And yet here she was, making a fool of herself, offering herself up on a plate, just to be rejected. Again.

'Wait! Giada!'

She only stopped because she'd reached the car, so she whirled round to look at him. 'Why? So you can reject me again?'

The driver's side door blasted open and Maria was there, her hand at her hip, ready to grab her weapon, eyes darting from Lucas and then back to Giada. 'Your Highness? Is everything all right?'

'Yes, it is, Maria. We're just…' Lucas glared back at Giada's right-hand woman, breathing hard and fast. If he was shocked at Maria's readiness to intervene, he didn't show it.

'What exactly are we *just* doing, Lucas?' Giada asked him, unable to keep the anger out of her voice.

'I need to talk to you. In private.' He glowered at Maria and then back at Giada. Neither of them moved. Something flickered behind his eyes. 'Oh, hell. Okay. Giada, come. Now.'

'Where?'

He took her hand and tugged her back towards the restaurant, then swerved sharp right to the secret cove. Before they'd even managed to close the gate he pushed her gently back against a tree.

'Gigi.' His hands cupped her face. 'Come back to me. Come back.'

'Who?' she threw at him. 'The Silly Princess?'

'No. You're not. You're… God, I can't even say it. I'm so…damned tied up.' He closed his eyes and she could see the struggle in him. She knew how hard it was for him to let go of his control. How he feared rejection so much that he was always so buttoned up. How he feared what might happen tomorrow so he wouldn't take the best from today, from her.

But then he stroked her hair back from her face and looked deep into her eyes. And just like that very first time, she saw him make his decision, saw the clarity and need in his gaze.

'I want you. *My* Gigi, not the polite public face. I want you. The real Gigi. The one with heart and soul. The one who cares deeply, who fights fiercely. The one who loves fun and wants nothing more than to enjoy life, and why not?' He shook his head as if realising something for the first time. 'Why the hell not take what we can, when we have the chance? We don't know what's around the corner.' He took her bandaged arm. 'Or when something bad might happen. Grab that chance, right? With both hands.'

My Gigi. Her heart squeezed. These angry moments were raw and ugly but each one brought them closer and closer. He just needed to stop fighting it. They both did. What they had was something she'd never experienced before, something intense and imperfect and yet beautiful and wonderfully wild. Who knew if she would ever have it again?

She pressed her palms, both the good one and the sore one, against his cheeks and laughed. 'I'm here. Your Gigi. And I'm not going anywhere until you've kissed me.'

'I can't… I can't stop this… I try to hold back but I can't. It's like there's an invisible force compelling me towards you. I thought I'd got over it after you left but you walked back into my ER and bang! Here it is again.'

Then there was no more talking because he slid his mouth over hers and her body almost exploded with desire. How could she feel this way about someone who was so utterly different from her? So wrong in so many ways? How could she want so much from him? With him?

But he saw her. Knew her. Saw beyond her title and her money, saw the real Gigi, and he wanted her.

His kisses brought her home, made her new. She wanted…oh, she wanted so much. Everything. She wanted to feel him against her, on her. In her. Wanted and wanted and wanted until she thought his kisses and his touch would never be enough.

His hands moved over her body, slipping the flimsy straps of her dress over shoulders, freeing her breasts so he could suck her nipple.

'Yes,' she moaned, arching her back at the sensation of his wet mouth on her tender skin.

Dio. She wanted his mouth everywhere.

She reached through the space between them so she could cup him, stroke him.

He groaned into her hair. 'Are you sure this is safe?'

'I'm not going to get pregnant, because I already am.' She laughed. 'Surely a doctor should know that?'

He raised his head and his gaze snagged hers, so intense, so true. Raw hunger filled his eyes. A desire so pure and bright she felt it in her soul. And then he smiled…not just his mouth but his whole face, his body, shrugging off that stern tightness. 'I need to be inside you, Gigi. I meant… is there a chance anyone can see us here?'

'It's dark. No one apart from Maria knows we're here. And Angelo, possibly, if he's seen my car is still here.' She clamped her arm around his neck as he made to step away from her. 'Don't go.'

'There's nowhere I'd rather be than with you.'

But she knew that wasn't true. Sure, for tonight he'd stay, but he'd go back to Seattle soon enough. But they had tonight. They had this.

'But…' He kissed her again, hard, then stroked her face. 'I am not going to put you at risk of being caught out here with me, doing the kind of things I want to do to you.'

'Lucas,' she moaned as her imagination ran riot. 'I don't care about being caught.'

'I do. This is not my private beach, it's some-one else's. We don't know who we can trust.'

'But Angelo is…' Not wanting the magical spell to break, she nibbled Lucas's ear. And from her own bitter experience she knew well enough not to trust anyone. 'I just love it here. I'm sure—'

'We are going back to the palace.' He slipped the straps of her dress back onto her shoulders.

She grabbed his arm. 'I can't run the risk that between here and the palace you'll put your Captain Sensible head on and leave me all aching and frustrated.'

'I want you, Gigi. I will still want you at the palace. And tomorrow, and the day after. You make me want to be Captain Slightly Less Buttoned Up. Captain Spontaneous. Captain Devil May Care.' Laughing—such a joyous melodic sound coming from his throat—he crushed her against the bark, enslaving her mouth with deep, wet, hungry kisses.

When she drew breath she giggled, pressing her body against his to feel the outline of his erection against her thigh. Wishing they were naked. Wishing he wasn't Captain Sensible trying very hard to be someone he wasn't. But she liked him all the more for trying for her sake and she knew she could only push him so far. She wiggled against his erection, making him groan. 'Captain Seriously Sexy.'

'Who is taking you back to the palace. We are going to bed. But don't worry…' he traced a fingertip down the front of her dress, between her breasts, making her shiver in anticipation '… I am not going to let you sleep for a very long time. Do not argue.'

He linked his fingers in hers and walked her back to the car. 'How fast can Maria drive this vehicle?'

'I'll ask her to step on it.'

She could barely breathe, feeling the heat of his body next to hers, knowing he wanted to be inside her…wishing he was. But when he slipped his hand out of her grip and stroked her thigh, bunching her dress in his fist so he could access higher and higher, she thought she was going to die of frustration and need. They couldn't get home fast enough.

As they walked through the front door the security guard nodded. 'Goodnight, Your Highness.'

'Goodnight, Enrico.' She waved, upping her pace. Bedroom. Now.

Lucas fell into step behind her, following her up the grand staircase. They passed one of the housekeepers, who gave a little bow. 'Sleep well, Your Highness.'

'You too, Nicole.'

It wasn't until they'd turned the corner into the empty corridor leading to the Napoli suite that Lucas caught her hand again. 'Is there ever a moment when this place isn't like Piccadilly Circus? Where have all these people come from?'

She laughed. 'They live here.'

'You have no privacy. Ever.'

She remembered how they'd made love in his bath, in his pool, in his kitchen, not having to worry about being seen, and wished they were free to roam around her house, doing the same. She sighed against him. 'It's my life.'

'I don't know how you live with so many people underfoot all the time. I value my freedom too much.' He shook his head. He didn't want this kind of life, that was obvious.

But he did want her.

They reached the door to his suite and she hesitated. He tugged her into the shadows, pressing his mouth to her throat. 'I don't suppose there's one of those secret corridors between here and your rooms?'

'Indeed there is. Why do you think I suggested you stay in this particular suite?' She giggled against his chest, breathing in his scent of something wild and male that drove her crazy with desire.

'I love how you future-proofed my stay.' He grinned.

She shrugged, her fingers playing across the neckline of her blouse. 'What can I say? I'm an eternal optimist.'

'Is it easy to find? In the dark?' The growl in his voice drove her sexual hunger up a notch.

'Oh, Captain Sensible, I'm turning you! You love this cloak and dagger life, right?'

'If it means I get to undress you again, then yes.'

'It's just there.' She pushed open the door to his suite and pointed to a panel in the wall. 'I'll come to you.'

'You'll come with me. Over and over.' He pushed her hair back and kissed behind her ear. 'You have sand on your cheek, Princess Gigi.'

'I'll shower.'

'No,' he growled. 'We can do it together.'

She was nervous. Stupid, considering they'd done this before. Even more stupid because she was carrying his child and they were connected in so many ways. But there it was. She wanted to be perfect for him, but her legs shook a little as she descended the steps between her rooms and his. What if…what if this wasn't perfect? What if she let herself fall under his spell, gave him her heart and he stamped on it?

But no, she told herself. Captain Sensible wouldn't do that.

She wouldn't let him. She'd take tonight but she'd keep her heart safe. And she would never ever trust a man. Never again.

But sex? Scratch that insatiable Lucas itch? Hell, yes.

She knocked quietly but there was no answer. 'Lucas,' she whispered as she pushed open the panel and stepped into his room. And, wow…in the few minutes she'd been upstairs he'd transformed the place into a soothing soft space lit by myriad candles. 'Lucas?'

The sound of running water drew her to the bathroom and she found him there, testing the temperature of the water in the large gilt sunken bath. More candles filled every space, every shelf, and bathed the suite in a golden magical glow.

He'd removed his shirt but his trousers were still on. Her eyes slid over the naked skin and she sighed at the sight of the corded muscles she'd committed to memory three months ago, itching to span them with her hands.

He turned. Saw her. Stilled.

It felt as if time stopped, the whole world stopped, as they looked at each other. He said nothing, but his heated eyes spoke volumes. No need to be nervous. He liked what he saw—just a barefoot woman in a simple silk sheath dress. And very expensive underwear…although he didn't know that yet.

His gaze heated her, made her feel exposed and yet desired. Adored. Craved. Her skin prickled in anticipation of his touch. She raised her chin, an act of defiance. *You want me, but I will have you.*

She was a princess, he was a successful ER consultant with more letters after his name than she could count, but in here they were equals. Lovers.

She shivered. His pupils dilated and he took a step towards her.

'I always did like this room,' she said, just to break the heavy lust-laden silence.

'Almost as fine as the bedroom.' He closed the distance between them and palmed her cheek, his fingers damp and cool. 'Hello, Gigi.'

'Hello, Lucas.' Unable to resist touching him, she brushed her fingers across the smattering of dark hair on his chest, ran her nails up to his throat, palmed the back of his neck and tugged his face down to hers.

'God,' he groaned, his mouth centimetres from hers. 'No small talk?'

'Have I ever said that you talk too much?'

'Maybe—'

'Too much talking and not enough kissing.'

She bridged the gap between them, crushing her mouth to his, giving no more space for thought. Just touch. Skin and heat and wet and hot.

Deepening the kiss, he slid his tongue into her mouth, exploring, hungry. She raked her fingers across his back, his shoulders, his arms, spanning those muscles, desperate to touch every inch of him. Wanting him inside her, filling her.

He pulled her dress over her head, consigning it to the floor, then he unclipped her bra, letting her breasts fall free. Groaning in appreciation, he cupped them, playing his fingers over her nipples, softly at first then harder until her breasts ached and her nipples peaked at his touch. A soft hurt that she didn't ever want to stop.

He propelled her backwards to the vanity, lifted her to sit on the edge of the counter, pulled her legs either side of him, grasped the curve of her hips and rocked her against him.

Hard. So hard.

'Trousers. Please. Off,' she managed through desperate kisses, and he obliged, discarding the chinos and boxers. Then he was in front of her, solid and steady and strong. And ready.

She took him in her hand and stroked his length, watching the mist descend in his half-closed eyes.

'Gigi.' It was a growl. A warning. A sigh, as he grasped her wrist. 'I—'

She rubbed against his erection. 'I need you. Please.'

'But I had so much planned.'

'Later. After. More. I just need you now. Lucas.'

He kissed her again, greedy, rough kisses as he settled in front of her, pulling her to the very edge of the counter, pulling her to the edge of her control, holding her close, pressing his body against hers until she felt his imprint everywhere, his scent…everywhere.

This man who was a danger to her equilibrium, this man who would leave her.

This man who understood what she needed, where she wanted his touch, where her body ached to be kissed, stroked. This man.

Then he was sliding inside her, filling her, his fingers slipping into the apex of her legs, stroking her most sensitive part as he slid inside, over and over. Stroking and sliding. Fast and deep.

His thrusts slowed and he opened his eyes and captured her gaze. This man who had changed her future, changed her life in so many ways. He stroked her cheek with a tenderness that squeezed her heart and made it ache.

He kissed her long and slow, angling his hips to thrust deeper until she knew nothing more than this sensation, this kiss, this man, this pleasure mounting inside her, over her, through her.

As the sensation became almost too much she gripped his shoulders, his name on her lips over and over. Then he rocked harder and faster inside her, filling her completely, until she felt his release throb through her, taking her with him.

His eyes locked onto hers, his gaze honey and whisky, golden and hot. 'Gigi. *God*, Gigi.'

And she knew soul deep that this man was hers. At least…for now.

She was wrapped around him, tight and hot, her mouth on his shoulder, her legs around his waist. His hip dug into the sharp edge of the vanity unit and he was getting cramp in his left leg but he couldn't think of anywhere else he'd rather be, even though he did not like this palace with its legion of staff and lack of privacy.

His breathing came in gasps and he couldn't find words. After all his efforts not to do this again, he'd done it. And he didn't care, because he'd been honest when he'd said there was no-where he'd rather be than with her. If only they didn't have to sneak around. If only they were free to be themselves, together. A—his chest hurt at the thought—family.

But that was impossible. He'd never wanted it, and yet when he was with her he wanted everything.

He held her tight against him, stroking her back, kissing her as she came down from her orgasmic high. When she was breathing normally again he unpeeled her from his skin and kissed her softly. 'This can't be comfortable.'

'Oh, you know. It's slightly more comfortable than wearing that floss masquerading as underwear.' She grinned and nipped his earlobe between her teeth.

He peered at the scraps of lace on the floor and frowned. 'That was your underwear?'

'Very expensive underwear.'

'I'll buy you some more. Lots. Just so I can rip it off you.'

'You have the best ideas.' She laughed, a wonderful perfect sound that brightened his heart even more.

'Yes. Yes, I do. You are one of the best ideas I've had.' He untangled her legs from his and stepped away, his eyes catching the soft swell of her belly. His own gut contracted. 'Damn, Gigi. I didn't even think. Did I hurt…? Are you okay?'

She smiled, spanning her stomach with her fingers. 'Absolutely okay. Do you want to…?'

She reached for his hand and drew it towards her, then pressed it against skin that was as soft as the silk dress he'd torn off her. He couldn't find words as he stroked across her belly. Emotions bundled up inside him, hitting him hard in the chest. This tiny swell was his baby. Theirs. It was real and happening.

He lowered his head and kissed just below her belly button. Tears pricked his eyes. Hot damn. He blinked quickly, making sure to keep his head bowed so she wouldn't see this reaction. He never cried. Ever. And he wasn't going to start doing it now.

'Lucas?' She tugged him up to look at her, concerned eyes scanning his face.

The feelings inside him were strange, unfamiliar. As if his heart was growing with a swell of pride and something else he couldn't remember ever feeling. And a good dose of panic too. He would be responsible for this tiny human for the rest of his life. And responsible for Gigi too. Because they were inexorably linked, tied to each other for ever. 'I will never let anything bad happen to either of you. I promise.'

But he had no more time for thinking when her mouth sought his again. This time it was greedy, possessive, a kiss deeper and longer and better than any other. A kiss of longing and want that bruised his heart, branded him as hers.

Eventually he lifted her from the counter and walked over to the bath, lowering her gently into it. 'Now, do I get to do all those things I had planned?'

'Totally.' She splashed water at him, similar to that first day in late summer. 'Join me?'

He didn't need to be asked twice so he slid in opposite her, the warm water easing his bones, although the tension he'd been carrying since they'd arrived in Isola Verde seemed to have already disappeared. He slid under the water then came up to see her watching him with a curious expression. 'What?'

She smiled. 'If I'd known how badly you've been missing work I'd have shoved you into that hospital the minute we arrived.'

He laughed. 'I'm sorry I've been a pain to live with.'

'I have you back, that's all that matters. Captain Sensible's gone rogue. Again.' After kissing him, she turned and backed up so she was leaning against his chest.

He reached around her, hugging her closer, kissing her neck, her head. His chest almost burst with lightness as he palmed her breast. Was this for real? 'I can't get enough of you.'

'Lucas…' She turned, planting a kiss on his nose then following up with foam bubbles. 'You already have all of me, and more.'

Sure he did. Right here, in this bath, in the palace, in the country he didn't live in and in secret.

He had her, yes. The difficult question was: for how long?

CHAPTER TEN

'IT'S A BEAUTIFUL MORNING. The sun is shining; it's so pretty. I know how much you love the island in the winter. We have the trees all decorated and it feels very Christmassy. When you get better we can walk in the gardens.' Gigi slapped her hand on the breakfast table. '*Stupido!* I never say things like that. Because we never walk together. Why am I even bothering? Okay. Okay.'

She took a deep breath, deleted everything and tried again, pressing 'Record' on the audio app on her phone. *Take forty-five.* 'Oh, Papa, this is so hard. I barely talk to you face to face, never mind via a phone app.'

She stared out of the window and watched the lightning shadows of his horses galloping through the trees.

'I hate to think of you lying there with all those machines around you, and with Dom not even being able to admit he's your son. I wish I'd tried harder, Papa. I wish you'd loved me as much as I love you. I wish we could have been a proper family, instead of having so much distance between us. And I wish I could have trusted you enough to tell you about Leandro and how he was trying to blackmail me. I wish I hadn't made that mistake in the first place but, well… I was lonely and he was fun at first.'

Lucas had been the polar opposite to Leandro. He'd been serious and uninterested in her and immediately she'd thought he was different. That was what had attracted her to him. His steadiness. His honesty.

She smiled at the thought of him. How many times had they made love in the last ten days? She'd lost count. Funny, she'd thought he'd hightail it back to Seattle as soon as he could break out of here but he'd stayed. Although she had a feeling he wasn't here just to support her—the hospital work was part of the draw too.

'I wish I could tell you about Lucas too…it's actually really difficult. I don't know what to do. I like him. I mean, I like him a lot. I'm having his baby, did you know that? Of course you don't. We all keep secrets from each other. He's…he's lovely. You'd like him. Although if Dom hears about what we've been doing he might just kill him.' She shook her head at the thought of all the complications this relationship brought with it— was it a relationship? 'But, *Dio*, it's nice to have someone here to keep me company instead of rattling around the place on my own like I normally do. I don't think you realise how lonely it is here for me.'

The door opened and Lucas breezed in. 'Hey, Gigi. You got up early.'

'Lucas.' She fumbled, trying to click off the app, almost dropping the phone in the process, which made it look as if she was doing something she shouldn't. She laughed, trying to cover up her sudden awkwardness. 'Um… You heard that?'

'Just a muffled sound. Nothing really.' He brushed a kiss on her head then helped himself to pancakes and berries.

She breathed out. *Phew.* 'I'm trying to record another message for Papa, but I still feel silly talking into a machine.' She pressed the 'Delete' button and then looked at him. 'Binned that attempt too. I think I'm up to take forty-six today.'

He smiled, popping a berry into his mouth and putting a plate of food in front of her. 'Eat. I know you won't have and you need to. You're doing great. Just say what you feel. Tell him what's going on in your life.'

'I don't think Papa wants to hear about my everlasting nausea. Or about our child. Or about us. I'm basically hiding my whole life from him at the moment.'

Lucas's eyes widened at the mention of *us*.

'Just tell him what the weather's like, that kind of thing.'

The recordings weren't supposed to be a confessional, then. It had been a weird kind of therapy, though, just saying her feelings out loud.

Lucas looked out the window. 'This place still confuses me, even after two tours. Remind me, where's King Roberto's suite?

'In the Verde Wing at the other side of the palace.'

'And Dom's?'

She pointed towards the central dome and beyond. 'Gathering dust over in the East Wing.'

'So you generally mooch around here on your own?'

Had he heard her say she was lonely?

The last thing she wanted was him analysing that. 'I have Maria and my staff. Friends you haven't been introduced to yet. Growing up, Dom and I shared the nursery and then I moved into the Bella Vista wing. Oh, I spoke to him earlier and he mentioned something about the charity ball at your hospital on the twelfth and do I want to go?'

'Oh? Interesting.' Lucas frowned and she could see guilt slither back into his features. 'He texted me this morning, too.'

Coincidence? Giada's heart hammered. 'Do you think he's suspicious about where we are?'

'I don't think so. It was just a friendly You're missing some fun times in the ER text. Fairly sure it wasn't fishing for information…at least not in relation to you. More about when I'll be back.'

'And are you going to the ball? Back to Seattle?' She'd known he would because he'd mentioned the charity event before they'd set off to come here.

An ache crept under her ribcage. This lovely bubble would burst the minute he stepped onto his plane and then she'd lose him to his life there. She'd tried to shield herself, of course, but he'd been too all-consuming to ignore.

As she expected, he nodded. 'Of course. It's the biggest charity event of the year and duty calls. I asked him to grab me a ticket. Are you going to go?' He caught her gaze. Paused. Then, 'Do you want to come? As in…*with me*?'

Her chest bloomed with warmth and excitement. 'Lucas Beaufort, are you asking me on a date?' So far, over and above their public outings, their intimate *getting to know you* had been in the confines of each other's suites.

He grinned, scraped his chair back and came around to her side of the table. He pulled her up, twirled her round, sat down and pulled her onto his knee. His mouth found hers and his kiss was filled with promise. Interesting, after an already *busy* kind of night. He was insatiable. *Grazie Dio.* 'It'll have to be an incognito date.'

'The best kind.' She grinned. 'And I can see Papa too. That will be wonderful. I'll make arrangements for my absence. Yes, I have to make formal arrangements, I can't just flit around like you do.'

'Will we tell Domenico?' His hands circled her waist under her blouse. 'About the baby?'

She shivered at his touch and in anticipation of where his hands would go to next. 'Not yet. After Papa's operation. But he'll definitely need to know before the announcement.'

'Announcement about…the pregnancy?' His hand stilled.

She thought about the way Bianca had looked at her the other week. 'I was thinking in the New Year. I can't just hide away until the baby is born, I need to be out working and I can't risk more gossip and speculation. Women instinctively know when other women are expecting—it's a thing.' At his raised eyebrows she said, 'They do, I promise. And, yes, just being the public face of the hospital is work for me. A royal endorsement brings in sponsorship. Outside the palace I'm always working. My life isn't my own. It belongs to the nation and…' he knew already but it had to be said '…so will our child's.'

Lucas looked as if he'd swallowed a lemon at

that, but he wasn't the only parent of this child; they both needed to learn how to compromise. She steeled herself against his reaction. 'I know, Lucas. I know, you have something to say about that too.'

But to her surprise he nodded. 'Okay. Yes. I understand. An announcement early in the New Year. This is real, isn't it?'

'Yes. It is.' She put his hand on her belly. 'I was thinking…'

'Oh, no.' His head shot up and he winced jokingly. 'Is that a good thing?'

'Always. You'll need to tell your parents too before the announcement is made.'

His mouth went flat and his eyes grew dark as he visibly shut down emotionally. 'No.'

'Lucas. Please. They need to know. I don't think you quite appreciate the media interest.'

'I've read the social media comments. I'm learning.'

'So you'll understand that your family will be bombarded by journalists. Their social media accounts will be scrutinised. They'll be followed, hounded. Even if you don't care what your family thinks about this child, you need to at least warn them about what's going to happen.'

'No.'

'Lucas. Please. It's not fair.' He didn't have to say that his parents hadn't been fair to him because she knew they hadn't. She turned round and straddled his lap. 'If I could erase any of what they did to you, I would. I hope this child will be the balm you need to believe that families can be a good thing.' His lip curled. She kissed it. 'I know you don't want a family, Lucas, but I guess…in some shape or form we will be one.'

And yet, despite knowing how much he didn't want a family, she kept having this image in her head of the two of them with a baby and it looked so…perfect. So…*everything*.

Impossible.

He stilled. 'How? How will we be a family?'

'We'll work it out.'

He blinked. Looked at his food then lifted her from his lap and sat her down next to him. There was a strange awkward silence as he filled a glass with orange juice. Did he even want to work it out?

Then his voice cut through her worried thoughts. 'Who is Leandro?'

'So you did hear.' So much for this being a beautiful morning. It felt as if all the happiness she'd been feeling for the last few days was suddenly sullied.

Lucas stared at the plate of food. 'Maybe a little.'

'Leandro is in the past.'

'I want to know what happened.' After the

emotionless response about his parents, this heated reply was interesting. He was all or nothing, a roller-coaster of emotions when it came to people he cared for and blankness to those who'd hurt him. Now his eyes blazed, which meant, she realised, he cared a great deal. 'Is he the one who blindsided you?'

Not wanting to remember that episode of her life, she blew out a breath. 'He was a big mistake I'd rather forget.'

'But not enough that you mention him to your father.'

She inhaled sharply. 'You heard it all?'

The lonely bit? The bit about her caring for him? Her heart hammered. He couldn't… She wouldn't… She didn't want him to know how much she liked him, and give him ammunition to hurt her in the future.

His eyebrows rose. 'I caught the tail end. Paulo stopped me in the corridor and asked about laundry. Then as he left I heard you talking. I didn't realise it was with your father. I didn't want to interrupt. Tell me about Leandro.'

'It's all been deleted anyway. Now you have to go to work.'

'Tell me, Gigi. I know every time you're thinking about him because I can see the pain and hurt in your beautiful face. Tell me. No secrets.'

'This is all a secret.' She waved her hand

around the room, finishing with her palm on his chest, wishing she could scream to the world that she'd spent ten wonderful days with Lucas.

'I meant...' He took hold of her hand. 'No secrets between us.'

So there was no escape, and he was right too: he'd been honest about his parents and that had helped her understand so much about him. Maybe, this way, he'd understand why Isola Verde was so important to her and why she was determined to do some good for her people.

She sighed, wrung her hands together and began. 'Leandro...was the ultimate life lesson. I met him in Naples at a party. He introduced himself as the son of an old aristocratic family. Good breeding, of course. I liked him. By which I thought he was hot... Oh, the craziness of youth only ever attracted by good looks and witty words. Turned out he was liar and a cheat and he played me.'

'A player played you?' Lucas's eyebrows rose. 'Wow, Gigi. I'm surprised.'

'You and me both. Turned out he was just a social climber who hadn't been honest about his background. We'd been dating a few months and then out of the blue he proposed. I was shocked, you know? We hadn't been serious; it had been fun but he wasn't special to me.'

She thought back to Lucas's proposal. Well,

hell, they were two completely different scenarios. One empty question but with a backdrop of roses and champagne and a private plane to Paris, the other an off-the-cuff panicked question in a Seattle bedroom with takeaway pizza.

But even though Lucas hadn't been wanting her to say yes, his proposal had at least been made with the best intentions. She sighed. 'When I said no, we were too young, it was too sudden, he became difficult, angry, threw things. Nothing violent towards me, but *because of me.*' She shuddered at the memory. 'This was one time I was relieved to have Maria in the next room. I had him thrown out of the hotel, told him I never wanted to see him again and thought that was the end of it, but it wasn't.'

'He threatened you? Hurt you?' Lucas's hands fisted.

'Not physically. A few weeks later I started to receive calls, no message or voice but replays of our conversations, of our…intimate moments. You know, the things you say when you're unguarded, when—you know, in the throes of passion.'

'There was a sex tape?' Lucas's lip curled and his eyes darkened.

Humiliation hummed through her. 'I don't know if there was a video. I don't remember anything about a camera…ever. But there was a recording and enough to tie that voice, those… sounds to me. Pretty soon texts came thick and fast, belittling me, repeating things I'd said about my father. Then there was a request for hush money.'

'Blackmail too?' Lucas looked at her in disbelief but there wasn't judgement, just shock.

She nodded, her mouth drying. 'I paid the first amount, but he wanted more. I refused. Then he said he'd sell the story to the local press, but that he wouldn't stop there.'

'Total jerk.' Lucas shook his head. 'Gigi, I am so sorry this happened to you. Not all men are like that.'

'I know.' She'd just allowed herself to be duped by the worst sort. 'I don't know if the sale was made. I managed to keep it quiet, well—between me, Maria and a big threat of Royal action and a court case. Plus, after a little digging into his background we had a few more things we could use against him. He eventually got the message that we were serious and I haven't heard from him since.'

Lucas stroked her cheek with the back of his hand. 'I am so sorry, Gigi.'

'Me too. I'd come so close to shaming my family, the Crown, the country. Remember, I already had a reputation as a troublemaker and party girl and Papa was at his wits' end. I was reeling from the lucky escape I'd had by managing to keep it from him, always being on tenterhooks that Leandro would somehow get the recording to him. I didn't know what to do; my head wasn't clear for a while. I was broken and felt like I was going around in a daze.

'Then, one day, I went for a drive around the city and passed the beautiful gardens that had been created in my mother's memory down in the old quarter. There were children playing, people enjoying the flowers and the sunshine, smiling, laughing in a space where she would always be remembered as someone special. She'd done so much for the community and was adored by everyone, and it got me thinking that all I'd ever created was pain and embarrassment. What was my legacy? Trouble, that's all. It hit me hard then… I didn't want to be remembered for yet another salacious gossip story; I wanted to create something I could be proud of.'

Lucas's eyes lit up as he joined the dots. 'The hospital.'

'Exactly.' She nodded. 'I dedicated a ton of time and energy to it and I'm damned proud of it. It was much needed and has already made a big difference to people's lives. And while I hate that portrait in the foyer, it reminds me how far I've come.'

'I can't even…' Lucas kicked his chair back

and stalked across the floor. 'Where the hell is that scumbag now?'

'Long gone and I don't care. You shouldn't either.'

'I want to punch him. I want to… Giada, I am so angry…'

He was so passionate about defending her, so ardent in his rage *for her*, it made her blood pound. She caught him and put her hands to his face. 'Lucas, you are magnificent.'

'I can't…' He shook his head, nostrils flaring as he swayed out of her hands. 'How could anyone treat you like that?'

'Because I let him. Because…' Her heart stung with the memory of embarrassment, self-hatred and the very sharp wake-up call that she could not be the Silly Princess any longer.

She'd never told anyone about this before, apart from Maria, of course. But saying it out loud was freeing and meant she could place it firmly in the past behind her. She knew she could entrust it to Lucas. Seeing his reaction, she knew he was on her side. 'I just wanted to be important to someone.'

He stared at her, so much empathy and affection in his eyes as he pulled her into his arms, wrapping her tight.

'Hell, Giada, you're important to me,' he whispered against her throat.

'Oh, Lucas.'

No one had ever said anything like that to her before. It was an understanding of who she'd been and how far she'd come. That she was worth something. He saw her, he heard her. He accepted her.

It was everything.

Something had shifted between them, something deep and profound. More, she knew it had taken him a lifetime to be able to say those words to someone. And he'd chosen her.

Her heart stuttered as she took his kisses and his ardent, passionate words.

And wished, with all her being, she could let herself believe him.

CHAPTER ELEVEN

Gigi smoothed down her dress as they stepped out of the cab in front of Seattle's famous Polar Club Hotel—the venue for the charity ball—and asked, 'How do I look?'

Breathtaking. Lucas held his hand out to steady her in her silver heels. 'You look radiant and beautiful. And if we weren't in the middle of Seattle I'd peel your clothes off and make love to you right here.'

'Tempting, although I'd freeze to death.' She laughed. 'Seriously, does this dress make me look pregnant?'

She was wearing an exquisite floor-length gown in the Isola Verdian regal colours of purple and silver, with a shimmering bodice, one shoulder bare, a nipped-in waist and a full skirt. Her hair was pulled up as it was in her portrait and there were diamonds worth hundreds of thousands of dollars dangling from her ears.

His chest hurt every time he looked at her...a good hurt, an ache he wanted to never wane, whether she was wearing jewels and finery, jeans and his old T-shirt, or absolutely nothing.

He inhaled the icy night air that was a far cry from the temperate climate where he'd spent the last couple of weeks. But he didn't give a damn about the weather; his sole focus on getting through this evening when he couldn't touch her, and without betraying himself to his best friend, because… Secrets.

They started to climb the white stone steps.

'No way am I commenting because, whatever I say it will be the wrong thing.' He leaned closer to her. 'And, for the record, I prefer you wearing nothing apart from me.'

'Lucas!' she whispered, her cheeks burning. She let go of his hand. 'We have to behave.'

'What can I say? You've unleashed a beast.' He'd grown too used to having her to himself, of stripping her naked whenever they were able to slip through the secret corridor… Decorum had slipped from his vocabulary.

But underneath the joky facade his gut was a tight ball of stress. There were so many people buzzing around—people he worked with, people he worked for; there were bound to be questions about what his family crisis had been about and where he'd spent the last two weeks. And he wasn't sure how he was going to answer any of them.

Tonight was the end of the bubble they'd been living in for the last few days. Days that had been shaped by work and fun and sharing more than he'd ever shared with anyone else. Weird, really, because he'd never imagined enjoying the intimate life that smacked of family and belonging, but he had. And now reality was crashing down.

As if she could read his mind, Gigi gave his arm a squeeze. 'Relax, Lucas, you're all coiled up. It'll be fine. Dom won't suspect a thing. Plus, you're back in Seattle now. Work tomorrow.' He wondered if he imagined the flicker of sadness in her eyes, but then she smiled, putting her palm to her chest as they entered the Aurora Dome room amid the loud chatter. 'Oh, this is lovely.'

He looked upwards. 'Almost as impressive as your palace.'

She followed his gaze to the huge stained-glass domed ceiling that had been lit up in festive colours, her eyes sparkling almost as much as the chandeliers and the crystal glassware on white–linen-covered tables. 'You haven't seen us do Royal properly, Lucas. Trust me, that is something to behold. But this is simply stunning. Oh, there's Max Granger. At least, I think it's him. He looks very like the man I spoke to on video calls. I need to speak to him about Papa.'

Wishing they were still back in his house, naked, exploring each other again and again,

Lucas followed her through the throng of party-goers towards the tall man loitering by the bar, and shook hands with him as Gigi introduced them.

Max smiled at Giada. 'I heard you visited your father today.'

'I went straight to the hospital from the airport. He looks so…vulnerable.' She nodded, her eyes darkening but her back straight and smile in place. To anyone else she would appear perfectly composed, but Lucas could see she was hiding her pain. 'I've been talking to him, but it's hard to know if he hears me.'

'All the research says patients respond more positively to treatment if they hear a loved one's voice,' the neurosurgeon said. 'He's doing well. We have a scan booked first thing tomorrow morning and if all is as good as we hope it is, we can proceed with the tumour surgery as planned on the fifteenth.'

'That is great news. Thank you.' Her hand fluttered at her throat and he wondered if her veneer of calm was starting to shatter. But she held it together. 'I'm so sorry to have interrupted your evening with work business, Mr Granger.'

'Not a problem.' Max smiled reassuringly, then his eye settled on a dark-haired woman in a long green dress walking towards them, and his attention to their conversation seemed to wane. He took a step away. 'Enjoy the ball, Your Highness,' he said, his voice low so no one around them could hear. 'Make sure to save room for the dessert. London Fog cake. You'll be blown away.'

'How would he know about dessert? We haven't even had the starters yet.' Gigi asked once Max had walked away.

Lucas shrugged. 'Must have insider info.'

'Who cares? It sounds amazing.' Gigi rubbed her stomach. 'I'm definitely having some.'

Lucas watched her and smiled, straddling the eternally difficult question of whether he should point out to her that when she flattened the fabric of her dress over her abdomen she did indeed look a little…rounder? But a female voice came from behind, *sotto voce*, saving him from that particular minefield. 'Excuse me, Princess Giada?'

Gigi turned, frowning. 'Yes?'

The hospital's new Head of PR—the dark-haired woman who Lucas thought may have distracted Max—stepped forward. 'I'm Ayanna Franklin. I've been dealing with your office regarding your father's accident.'

'You're Ayanna! Good to meet you.' Gigi shook Ayanna's hand. 'Thank you for working so hard to keep this all under wraps. I know you've been busy.'

'Learning the ropes, to be honest. I'm new in the role but what with having VIP guests at the hospital and organising this ball I've hit the ground running. You have no idea how difficult it is sourcing London Fog cake for this many guests.' Ayanna grinned. 'I really hope you love it.'

'I'm sure we will.' Lucas nodded. 'Sounds delicious.'

'It certainly does,' Gigi joined in. 'Max was just talking about it.'

'Max was?' Ayanna's eyes widened in what looked like panic.

Lucas clarified, 'Max Granger. Yes. Do you know him?'

'Er…we've met. Yes.' Ayanna's cheeks flamed and he was left contemplating what was going on between the neurosurgeon and the PR director. Given his own secrets, he pushed it to the back of his mind. None of his business.

Gigi replied, snapping him out of his thoughts. 'Well, Ayanna, I can't thank you enough for helping us at such a difficult time.'

It astounded him that she was able to be so animated and gracious after a twelve-hour flight followed by two hours at her father's bedside. She astounded him, full stop.

Having finished her conversation, Gigi turned to him but something, or rather someone, caught her eye. She raised her hand in a small wave and muttered out the side of her mouth, 'There's

Logan, our old bodyguard. AKA your new trauma surgeon. I can't remember whether I'm supposed to know him or pretend I've never seen him before… I've got baby brain. Oh, he hasn't seen me anyway. Maybe I'll catch up with him later.'

'How is it that I work here and yet you know more people than I do?' Lucas laughed as he scanned the crowd, seeing nothing but a sea of faces, suits and sparkling jewels. The chatter was reaching epic volumes against the backdrop of an orchestra playing classical music. There was an excited buzz and he had no doubt the hospital charity was going to raise a lot of money tonight. 'Gigi?'

He waited for a response but she'd paled a little and her whole body seemed to freeze. She touched Lucas's arm. 'There's Dom. Should we…?'

No. His gut tightened and his first instinct was to run, but that was certainly not what he was going to do. That would only increase suspicion. 'Sure. We have to do it sometime.'

'Okay. Keep your distance, we're friends, that's all.' She gave him a conspiratorial wink. 'Remember, no one knows I'm Dom's sister.'

'Yes, Your Highness,' he ground out through gritted teeth, not wanting to keep his distance at all. Not wanting to be here at all. 'This is going to be awkward on so many levels.'

Luckily, Dom was standing with their colleague, orthopaedic surgeon Emilia Featherstone, and the small talk between them all was general, brief and light before they were called to dinner.

Even though they were seated at the same large circular table as Dom and Emilia, they were separated by other guests, far enough away for intimate conversation to be difficult, particularly in front of the other six diners with them. But the sharp ache under Lucas's ribcage didn't fade at all. He'd got away without interrogation this time, but it was going to happen. And either he was going to have to lie or front up to his best friend very soon.

He breathed out, grateful for a reprieve, and tucked into a particularly delicious Caprese salad reminiscent of Isola Verdian cuisine.

'Do you think he suspects anything?' Lucas asked Gigi, glancing over towards his friend.

'I think he's barely registered that we're here. He's only got eyes for Emilia.' Giada watched her brother whisper something to Emilia. 'How did he put it? Old friends? I bet there's something more going on there.'

'Do you think so?' He had to admit that they did look cosy. Had something been going on that he didn't know about? Were Emilia and Dom involved? He was starting to think he didn't know his best friend at all.

Giada swallowed. 'That dress is something else, she looks amazing. No wonder he's distracted.'

'It's red, yes. Kind of nice. But not a patch on yours.' He meant it. She was the most beautiful woman in the room.

'You really don't have to say that.'

But he could see her heart wasn't in this conversation as her eyes kept darting to her brother. Lucas realised that, unlike him, she wanted to talk to Dom. 'I'm sure he'll make an effort to talk to you properly later.'

'You think so? When he has a beautiful woman at his side? Domenico is smitten.' There was no bitterness in her tone, although it was a little wistful and resigned to the fact that Dom had other things on his mind than his sister. Again.

Lucas's heart stung for her. All her life she'd been wanting someone in her family to notice her. He couldn't fathom how they hadn't—she was dazzling in every way. 'There's been no evidence of any kind of relationship between them, other than collegial friendship, for as long as I've known them. I'm sure it's just a coincidence they were chatting when we went over. Anyway, it's none of our business.'

'It is very much my business if she's going to become Queen of Isola Verde.'

Okay. He hadn't thought about that. 'I'm really not sure that's on her agenda. She loves being a doctor. I can't see her giving that up. I doubt Emilia even knows Dom's real identity.'

'If she does know, it's because Dom thinks she's special. Look at the way he's gazing at her.' Gigi drank her sparkling water, her gaze returning to Lucas. 'You don't have to see the ramifications but I do.'

'Oh, I see them all right. We only had a very quick chat with them and even then I stuffed up. Did you see Dom's eyes narrow when I called you Gigi? And then I said Isola Verde is beautiful and I'm not supposed to have been there.' He hit his head with the heel of his hand. 'I am so not good at lying.'

'Yes, you are. When you're on duty you mask your emotions and it's just the same for me. You learn very quickly not to let things affect you, and if they do you simply cover your reactions with a smile.'

He much preferred the animated, emotion-filled Gigi. The one he'd made love to just before she'd put on that sexy dress. The one who'd cried out his name while stealing his heart. Damn, he wished they weren't here right now, playing grown-ups when they could be at his house, playing an entirely different game.

But all this talk about Domenico and the King reminded him that this affair with her was fast coming to a conclusion. Soon the truth would be out about Roberto's operation—they certainly couldn't hide it for ever and, whatever happened to the King, Dom would have to return to Isola Verde and take his rightful place there.

Gigi's pregnancy would be obvious. There would have to be an announcement and Lucas's part in this would break up his friendship with Dom.

What then for Gigi?

A flicker of hope lit up inside him. If Dom became King and returned to Isola Verde then Gigi would be off the hook there. She wouldn't have the burden of shouldering the monarchy's responsibilities like did now. Would she consider moving here? She'd be free to—

'Hey, Lucas.' Arvi, the paediatric endocrinologist on his right, leaned over, swirling his glass of red wine. 'Are you going to the Seahawks game tomorrow?'

'Er…no. Who are they playing?'

'Vikings. Gonna be a tough one. That new quarterback…'

Not wanting to be rude, Lucas applied the mask

of interest and immersed himself in football talk while his *date* chatted to the woman next to her.

Only she wasn't his date. He couldn't hold her hand, couldn't parade her onto the dance floor. He couldn't kiss her under the mistletoe someone had strung up, he couldn't cradle her belly and rock in time to the music. He couldn't announce to everyone that she was carrying his child, because that announcement had to be timed and worded carefully and sent out to the world's media, and he wasn't even sure his name would be mentioned.

Being with her these last few weeks had changed him. She'd taught him to look for the positives, to cling to hope. To make the best out of every situation. She'd made him laugh.

Simply, she'd made him happy.

He felt the brush of her leg against his and the rush of desire almost overwhelmed him. He slid his hand under the tablecloth and found hers. She turned her palm upwards and he stroked lazily over her skin, knowing where her sensitive places were and that his touch drove her wild. He heard her breathing quicken and felt her shift closer. As close as public decency would allow. They, like Domenico and Emilia, were old friends after all.

The first chance they had to get out of here he'd take it. If reality was going to be hitting them soon he wanted to live in the bubble for as long as he could, which meant tonight would probably be their last.

The main course was served. Beef. He was now involved in a conversation about new diabetes management technology. And almost dying of pure lust whenever Gigi turned to him and he got a glimpse of her smile, the waft of her perfume, the profile of her gorgeous breasts.

He was going mad. He couldn't stop thinking about her.

Somebody gave a speech about something... he wasn't focusing on anything but her.

Dessert was something fancy—a cake that tasted like Earl Grey tea with smoky grey icing, and indeed, as delicious as both Max and Ayanna had suggested it would be.

'Good?' Gigi asked as she swallowed her final piece before making a start on the rest of his.

'Amazing. More than amazing.' And he wasn't just talking about the food.

She'd twisted in her seat and was turned towards him now, her knees between his, her foot stroking his leg...all hidden by the long drape of the white linen tablecloth. Her hand crept over to his thigh.

He blinked. Swallowed. 'Gigi,' he warned, wishing he didn't have to say it. 'We're supposed to be behaving.'

'No one's here, Lucas. Look around, no one's interested in us and no one can see.'

He'd been so absorbed in her he hadn't realised that their table was empty, apart from themselves. Domenico and Emilia were on the dance floor and Gigi was watching them with a curious expression.

Judging by the way they were dancing so closely there was definitely something going on between his friend and the surgeon. And if there wasn't…there would be soon.

Lucky Domenico. No one knew his real identity here so he could wine and dine and dance and risk being the subject of hospital gossip for a little while…and then his life would change irrevocably when he was crowned King.

Lucky? Dom's life would never be his own again. Lucas was going to miss his friendship and camaraderie in the ER. Things wouldn't be the same.

A bit like his own life. Who would have thought he'd be at a charity ball with a princess rubbing his leg very close to his crotch?

God, he wanted her. Wanted more than this. Wanted everything. And the fact she'd opened up to him and started to trust him a little gave him hope that they could work this out somehow. As a family. The three of them.

Whatever that meant. Even the word made him panic, but he calmed himself. Others managed it.

He touched her hand, to stop it ascending to his trouser zip more than anything. Because he wanted to sink into her, hip deep, and he wasn't sure how tight a grip he had on his self-control. 'Do you want to dance?'

She shook her head and smiled, her fingers wriggling under his hand and tiptoeing upwards. 'Not the way I want to dance with you.'

His gut tightened in anticipation. He had the feeling of falling and he didn't want it to stop. 'You can show me later.'

'Oh, Captain Sensible, I will.' Her eyes danced and she scraped her chair back. 'Do you think it'd be rude if we left now?'

'I think it would be the best idea you've had in a long time.'

They barely made it from the taxi to his front door without kissing at every step. Which excited and frustrated her. She wanted him inside her, to scratch the itch that had been niggling her since she'd watched him dress in his tux earlier.

Eventually, he thrust his key in the lock and they tumbled through the door. Gigi laughed as he backed her up against the wall, her heart full of only him. 'Oh, wow, Lucas. Happy to be home?'

'I'm happy to be wherever I can strip your

clothes off…with my teeth.' He kissed her hard then pecked a trail across her collarbone and snagged her dress…with his teeth. 'You were driving me wild back there. All I wanted to do was sink into you.'

'That would give the bigwigs something to talk about.' She tugged his black bow-tie loose and let it fall to the floor. Shame. The man looked indecently good in formal wear, but he looked even better naked. Her fingertips slid inside his shirt and she tugged the crisp white linen out of his trouser waistband then slid her hand down to stroke his erection, enjoying the way he moaned against her hair. 'We missed the charity auction. Is that bad?'

His mouth was on her décolletage and tracking lower, his fingers unzipping her dress. 'I'm sure they'll make enough money without us.'

'Once the truth is out about Papa being here, I'll make a generous donation to Seattle General Hospital by way of a thank-you.' It *was* bad. It was selfish to want this and only this. To crave being with him, to have his skin against hers, to wrap herself in a cocoon of *us*. But it was all she could think of.

Lucas tore his mouth from her breast. 'We need to talk to Domenico. *I* need to—'

She silenced his words, her finger against his

lips. 'I do not want to think about my big brother when I'm doing this.'

'Good point. I want you. Here. Then we work out our plan.' The plan they'd been avoiding because they both knew it meant the end of this.

Or the start of something. Her face lit up. Maybe…?

He growled her name against her throat and tugged her into the kitchen, lifting her to sit on the counter, her dress forgotten somewhere on the hall floor. He stepped back and looked at her, his eyes sliding over her face then to her shimmery dove-grey strapless bra and matching panties. His gaze burned hot. Then he came closer and pressed first his palm then his lips to her bump. 'God, Gigi. You are incredible.'

'Stop looking and start doing,' she commanded, even though the way he made her feel with just a look was just as much a turn-on as his touch. Well…almost.

She wound her feet around his waist and pulled him to her, her skin, her everything straining for him. Not just for his touch but for him, the essence of him, the imprint of him against her skin, his taste. His heart.

Wordlessly he stroked her face, her throat, her breasts and lower, withholding kisses. Making her want and want and want. He smiled. 'I could look at you all day.'

'You'd get very bored very quickly.' She laughed and shook her head.

All day? All year? A lifetime? The thought stilled her. This. Him. For ever. It scared her. Excited her, too.

When she couldn't bear it any longer she cupped his face and pulled him to her, snatching wet, hot hungry kisses, tearing at his shirt and his trouser zip until he was stripped bare.

His hand glided from her glittery sandal up her calf, her thigh, and then he ripped her panties and laughed. 'Another set bites the dust.'

'Plenty more where they came from.'

'I prefer you without them anyway.' He sucked a nipple into his mouth, making her shudder with pleasure. 'I prefer you exactly like this.'

'What is it about you and counter tops?' She laughed as he pulled her to the edge of the granite, remembering their first time in his bathroom at home.

Her home, not his. The thought struck a chord of pain inside her. She was getting carried away on what-ifs when they still had so much to work out.

'Now who's talking too much?' His hand was on her cheek. 'I like to have you right here, because I love to see your face, Gigi. When…'

'When…?'

'Now…' he groaned as he slid inside her, eyes

locked on hers. 'Right there. That look. The mist. The joy. *Dio*, you are beautiful.'

'You spoke Isola Verdian,' she gasped, breath catching as sensation after sensation rippled through her. Hot. Dazzling. The light in her heart was swelling and growing. She clasped his shoulders. 'Lucas…'

He pulled her closer until there was nothing but skin and kisses and heat. And he moved and he moved and he moved. Long slow strokes that whipped her breath away and made her want more. Then she felt his pace change, angling differently, catching her…there.

And yes, yes. His grip tightened. She shuddered against him and he called her name into the darkness.

Dio. It was everything. *He* was everything. Her Lucas.

CHAPTER TWELVE

It took a few minutes for the world to come back into sharp focus, his heat and body still tightly holding her as if she was something precious he couldn't bear to let go.

Reluctantly she peeled herself away and laughed. 'Bedroom next time?'

'Everywhere, please. Although I'm not sure there's a room here that we haven't made love in.' He smiled, little beads of perspiration dotting his forehead, his breathing still heavy. 'We're free here, Gigi. No one to bother us, no sneaking around.'

Ah.

That was what he wanted, she knew. To be free. And she wasn't and could never be, unless she relinquished everything she knew and walked away from her royal life.

She kissed him again and slipped down from the counter, an ache settling deep in her chest. She rubbed her ribcage with the heel of her hand, but it didn't go, lingering even after they'd cleared up and slid under his cool linen sheets.

Within minutes he was asleep and she watched him for a while, stroking his back as she went over the day's events in her head. The low of seeing her father attached to those machines. Seeing Domenico looking happy. The sting of pain that they hadn't managed a proper conversation about things that really mattered. The high of Lucas in his finery, his laughter. Holding his hand, stroking his thigh in public…almost.

They never did get the chance to dance.

Thinking of her brother with a woman he clearly adored brought her own future starkly into focus. Because, for all Lucas's *I'm happy to be wherever I can strip your clothes off*, it just wasn't true, was it?

He didn't want to be tied by conventions and formalities, didn't like the palace—her home. Didn't like intrusions and distractions. Didn't like her life. Didn't, in fact, like the idea of a family. And it wasn't fair to foist all of that on him or to suggest he had to be part of it.

She was the Royal, not him. She was the one with her future fated. All he'd ever wanted was right here in Seattle. His lovely house, his amazing job, his friends. His life.

She couldn't be Mrs Sensible here in Seattle

and he really, really didn't want to live in Isola Verde.

But how could they co-parent across the world?

Her head hurt with the possibilities; none of them felt right. Her heart ached with the realities. With the way she'd allowed herself to feel something for Lucas when, even from the beginning, she'd known nothing would ever be possible.

Maybe she'd just have to be honest with herself, even if it felt as if she was tearing her own heart apart. She needed to put this firmly in a box. Lucas was a temporary thing. Like the others. He was a challenge she'd conquered.

But he'd conquered her too. Broken down her defences and made her his.

She didn't want to remember how his kisses made her feel as if she was drowning and she never wanted to surface. How he understood her like no one else ever had. How he saw her for who she was, and who she wanted to be. She didn't want to remember his touch, his low, rumbling, hard-to-earn laugh.

But she did. She remembered all of it, playing slowly around her head, haunting her, torturing her. Emotions zipped through her heart. It was too complicated. Everything was crashing in on her. If one of them got their way, the other would have to give too much. More than anyone should have to give, just to be together.

So maybe it was time—and kinder to both of them and, most importantly, to their child, who did not need parents who were together and unhappy, wearing masks to hide their real feelings.

Time to walk away.

Her side of the bed was empty when Lucas woke up, but, ever aware of her, he sensed her moving around the room. Still half-asleep, he lifted his head and scanned the semi-darkness. She was over in the corner, hair neatly tied back in a sleek ponytail, a pretty grey woollen dress and knee-high boots gracing her blossoming body. Not the gorgeously crumpled, sex-addled woman he'd held all night.

He yawned, shuffling up the pillows. 'What time is it?'

'Sorry. Did I wake you? It's seven-fifteen.' She gave him a tight smile and then bent again, her hands moving backwards and forwards over something he couldn't quite make out in the dim light.

'What are you doing, all dressed up and princess-like? And early? So early. Come back to bed.' Then his heart kicked into a weird beat, unsettled and jerky. Because he'd just worked out what she was doing.

Her voice was as tight as her smile. 'Lucas. I… We…'

She was folding up clothes and putting them into her case.

She was leaving.

Her shoulders sagged a little and she held an item of clothing close to her chest. 'I'm packing.'

He didn't understand. Tried not to anyway. The jerky heartbeat sped up. 'To go where?'

'Home.'

Not this home. Clearly. He threw back the sheets and dragged on a robe because he couldn't do this naked. He felt suddenly weirdly vulnerable and off balance for the first time in decades. Since he realised his family didn't want him. It was happening all over again. He tried to stay calm. 'But you've just got here, Gigi.'

'I know and it was an amazing ball, but now I have to go to the hospital to say goodbye to my father, then I have a plane to catch. I thought… I assumed you knew I'd go home after the ball.'

'At some point, yes. But not so soon. Not today. We barely slept.'

A sigh. 'It was wonderful, *si*? Now I have a car waiting.'

'No.' He stalked over to her, closing the lid on her suitcase. 'We can't carry on like this. We have to talk about these things. I need to know where I am.'

'You are here, Lucas, where you belong. I am going back to my home, where I belong. You know how things are there. We can't leave the place for long with no Royal presence.'

Panic gripped his gut. He'd been wilfully negligent in pushing the agenda because it had suited him, but what the actual hell? He pushed his fingers through his hair. 'What happens now?'

'When Papa is better and Dom is back home, then we can talk some more. I don't think...' She sank onto a chair, suddenly looking every bit as if she'd only had a couple of hours' sleep and needed much more. 'I don't think we're in a place to start making decisions about the future.'

Panic morphed into anger. Not at her but at their singularly stupid reality. 'So you thought you'd just up and go. If I hadn't woken up would you have even said goodbye?'

'Of course, Lucas. I was just sorting my things out.' The smile she gave him was completely devoid of any emotion and he saw it then. Saw the way she was emotionally withdrawing, the way she'd been taught. His gut went into freefall.

He wanted to shake her. 'For God's sake. Why are you acting like this?'

A stiff shake of her head. 'I'm not acting.'

'Hell, Gigi, I know you.' She was erecting walls, putting the barriers back in place. Sliding on that mask he'd seen her wear for other people but not for him. Not for them. She'd always been open and honest, her true self, and now that fun-loving Gigi had gone. 'Stop being that damned automaton. Come back to me, Gigi.'

'I'm sorry, Lucas.' She shook her head, all Princess Giada now. 'I have to go.'

She clicked the lock and then lugged the suitcase upright, wincing as she strained her damaged wrist. And, God help him, even though every part of him hated it that she was leaving, he gently moved her aside and grabbed the case. 'I don't know why I'm helping you, to be honest.'

'Because you're a good man, Lucas. Don't forget that.' She clipped downstairs and walked, straight-backed, to the front door.

She was really going. This was the end for them.

Pain bubbled up again, closing his throat, tripping his heart. She was actually leaving.

'Gigi…' He wanted to ask her to stay…for ever. He wanted her to promise never to leave him because he loved her, and if she loved him back then this could work. 'Can't we just—?'

'No. I have too much in my head, Lucas. I can't… Look, the taxi's here.'

He wanted to slam the door closed and wrap her in his arms. 'No. Gigi. We talk now.'

'And what? End up in a big fight? Achieve nothing but heartache? Best to just cut our losses right now, don't you think?'

'What about last night, the last two weeks? I

thought you...' Maybe he'd been kidding himself. Falling for her, believing she felt the same. When, let's face it, he was completely the wrong guy for her and they both knew that.

The ache under his ribcage intensified as he realised he hadn't just fallen for her, he loved her.

Whoa.

No.

That had not been the plan at all. Because she would not move here, he knew that. He'd seen her in her country, how much she loved the place and the people. How much she belonged there. Not here, not in this world.

And what then for their child?

The last couple of weeks they'd avoided discussing the realities, choosing instead to fall in love with the growing bump.

Falling in love. There it was again. The everpresent swell in his chest. The same for his child as for the woman carrying it.

He rubbed his forehead.

How could he have been so stupid as to allow himself to fall for her? He was on a trajectory that could only end in pain. She did not need him. Was not destined for someone like him.

In his experience, love was conditional on how you acted, whether you performed to a particular standard. Love could be cut off.

And yet he couldn't cut off this feeling now. Couldn't stop it.

He shook his head. He had to stop it. He had to draw a line in the sand. She was leaving, again. It would always be like this and he would know only hurt and dissatisfaction.

She was committed to one thing only: her country. He could see that now, could see her hands tightening on her handbag straps, the yearning of her body to get to the car.

He inhaled as she opened the door and the cold early morning air wove around them, an Arctic blast that made her blink fast.

Or was that because she was going? Was she fighting tears? But why? She was the one leaving.

Rejection was the one thing he wasn't prepared to accept again. He could walk away but he would not be pushed. He would not hear her say the words. Worse, he wouldn't wait in the silence wishing, wanting, praying to hear from her again and knowing it wouldn't happen. The way it had played out with his family. He had to have an equal say in a relationship; he couldn't be at someone's beck and call, only to be dropped when things got difficult or inconvenient.

He needed some control. 'I'll walk you to the car.'

'Thank you.' She almost looked grateful that he wasn't causing too much of a scene. 'Don't you dare think I'll cut off ties with you. This is your child and you will be part of its life.'

'Damned right I will.' He closed the car door, barely able to breathe. The pain in his chest spread outwards like a stain. 'I'll be in touch.'

She would not cry. She would hold her head up, fasten her seatbelt without letting him see how much her heart was breaking. It was the Baresi way.

Oh, God, Lucas. What am I doing?

She wanted to put her palm on the window, to open the door and run to him. Wanted to tell him how much she loved his kisses, his warmth, his laugh. How much she wanted things to work out but that she didn't know the formula to get there.

Not for the first time did she wish she wasn't a princess with duty and responsibility and a whole damn country to take into account every time she did a single thing.

Lucas Beaufort was the best thing that had happened to her and yet she was leaving. But saving herself was the only thing she could do. The car pulled away and she closed her eyes. She would not look back. Would not chase that dream. Because that was all it was—a lovely, impossible dream.

Her phone rang and she ignored it. But it rang again and again and eventually she pulled it out of her pocket. Domenico. Her heart leapt to her throat. So early?

His voice was grave and low. 'I've just spoken to Max. Gigi, it's not good news. I'm so sorry. Papa's tumour is growing.'

That was all she heard or understood. He said a few other things but everything blurred. All she knew was that she wished today wasn't happening.

A nurse met her at her father's bedside and explained that his intracranial pressure was rising. More scans were needed, more tests. Gigi sat and held her frail father's hand while chaos swam inside her. Everything was falling apart and she was being torn into a million pieces. And here again she had to wear that mask that said everything was fine. Just fine.

It wasn't.

'Do you know where Dr di Rossi is?' she asked the nurse, wanting a familiar face, someone who understood.

But the woman just shrugged and fiddled with her father's IV. 'I don't know. Probably in ER.'

Truth was, she wanted Lucas. She wanted to feel his strength and his warmth. To lean against his chest and have him stroke her hair.

Lucas would come if she asked him; he'd hold her hand and tell her everything was going to be okay. But she couldn't do that to him. He wasn't a plaything she could pick up and throw away at a moment's notice. Emotion throbbed in the centre of her chest.

She *needed* him. She put her hand to her belly and cradled their child. They needed him, more than ever, but she couldn't go back to him and ask. Not now.

So here she was facing the stark truth: her life was changing and there was nothing she could do about it. She was utterly alone.

Which, in some ways, was a good thing because that way no one would see she was crying.

CHAPTER THIRTEEN

HER FATHER WAS AWAKE!

It was the best Christmas present ever.

The last two weeks had been exhausting as she'd twice flown back from Isola Verde to sit by her father's side. He'd initially taken a sharp turn for the worse and Max had been unsure if he could remove all the tumour, or even if her father would ever wake up again. But he'd operated anyway, because there would have been no hope if he hadn't.

So she'd clung to positivity, staying at the Four Seasons, sneaking through Seattle General Hospital, avoiding Lucas at all costs, always worrying he might see her and force a conversation where she would cry or break down. And yet secretly wishing she could glimpse him to see if he was surviving without her.

She was barely clinging on without him.

Then it was back to Isola Verde to rule the country in her family's absence. Pretending she was fine, pretending this baby wasn't sapping her energy. Pretending her heart wasn't breaking.

But today, Christmas Day, she skipped through the hospital, because her father was awake and asking for her!

Christmas carols played as she walked through the ward. The staff waved to her—one was dressed as a Christmas fairy, another had a flashing Santa hat, and everyone wore smiles—but Gigi felt discombobulated by it all. What was she going to find? Was her father going to be okay? Would he even recognise her?

She kissed his cheek, ecstatic to see his dark Baresi eyes open, direct and alert, even though he was still clearly pale and fragile. She breathed out slowly. 'You look so much better than the last time I saw you, Papa.'

'Because you're here, my daughter.' He gripped her hand as she sat next to the bed.

Wow. She scanned the area for Domenico, simply because she wanted to check their father was actually okay. He'd never said words like that to her before. She ran her palm over the back of his hand, promising to say all the things she'd wanted to say to him, starting with, 'I love you, Papa.'

'I love you, Gigi. I'm sorry… I was not the father I should have been.'

'Hush, Papa. Don't talk like that.' Tears pricked her eyes. 'I did things I shouldn't have and I'm sorry. I'm so sorry. I was angry and hurt and I embarrassed us all.'

'No. It is my fault. I struggled with you. I was lonely and sad after your mother died.' He raised his fingers. 'I've been thinking a lot.'

'You were asleep a long time, Papa.' People didn't think while they were in a coma, right?

'Dreaming. Thinking… You were by my side at the Armistice parade every year. On the balcony, waving to the crowds on Alessandro Day, in the rain, in burning sunshine.' He gave her a weak smile. 'I believed our people were there for me and they were, but they were also there for you, Gigi.'

She couldn't swallow past the lump in her throat. 'They love you, Papa. We all do. So much.'

'And now you're here after representing the family at home. Holding everything together until I return. I didn't see you before, darling girl…' He clasped her hand to his chest. 'But I see you now.'

'Oh, Papa.' It was all she'd ever wanted: to be seen, heard, respected. To be loved by her family. She blinked fast to stop the tears. 'All I want is for you to be strong enough to come home.'

'We have to talk…'

'Yes, of course. When you're stronger.'

'Now.' His voice recovered some of the regal strength she knew so well. 'Domenico doesn't want to be King, I know that. He has a life here and, from what I hear, someone he wants to share a life with. But you, *bella* Gigi...you could be Queen.'

'What? Me? No. No, I can't.' The thought was ridiculous.

'You were born for it.'

'No.' *I'm pregnant. I can't do this. Not on my own.* The hurt at leaving Lucas hadn't diminished—in fact, it had got worse. She missed him. She wanted him back. She just couldn't be Queen. Couldn't be Queen and have Lucas at the same time. It was impossible. 'Domenico is Crown Prince and will ascend the throne after you. Anyway, you have years left in you.'

Her father slowly moved his head from side to side. 'I'm tired, Gigi. My head hurts. I don't know if my decisions are right or wrong. I don't want to second-guess myself. It's a new age, I haven't embraced things... I don't know social media. I don't know the young people, but you do. You were made to be Queen. I wish it to be so. And soon.'

'Papa.' Panic gripped her belly. 'What are you saying?'

'I'm too old and sick. Isola Verde needs to be ruled by a steady hand, by a monarch who wants to be there, by someone with a future. Dom doesn't want to go home, Giada. I don't want him to do something he doesn't want to do.'

None of this made sense. Maybe he was still confused from the operation. 'Domenico is to be king. We had a conference call with the palace earlier and the official announcement is to be made tomorrow morning.'

'No, Gigi. He does not want to be King. I know that. I saw that with my own eyes. He wants to live and work here.'

'But who will rule?'

'You will. Queen Giada.'

'I can't. I'm not—' She pressed her hand to her throat as panic bubbled inside her. Panic and…yes, some excitement too. It was contrary to the succession plan, but her father was right, she could do this. She'd been doing it for the last few months anyway. She'd held the family and the country together and it had felt…right. Her duty and her privilege.

But it would be the final nail in the coffin for her and Lucas.

Sadness choked her, mourning for what they could have had. But he hadn't reached out to her. Hadn't called. Domenico had said he'd barely spoken to him over the last couple of weeks. It was as if he'd cut himself off from the only family he'd ever had a chance to be a part of.

Her heart hurt at the loss. She missed what they'd had in those last two happy weeks in Isola

Verde. But she had to be strong now and make decisions not only for herself but for her child.

'You are everything our country needs. Please.' Her father stroked her hair, a gesture so tender it brought more tears. 'Do this for me. For us all.'

She cupped his hand and brought it to her cheek. 'I don't know what to say.'

'Say yes, Gigi.'

Oh, she wanted to. So much. 'But… I can't be Queen, Papa. I have news.' This was not how she'd planned to tell him. He'd given her the greatest gift and she was going to disappoint him again. She took a ragged breath through an aching throat. 'Papa… I… I'm pregnant.'

Her father closed his eyes and she was sure he cursed in Isola Verdian. But after a moment he smiled and squeezed her hand. 'You are always full of surprises, my darling.'

Her chest was holding back a sob but she couldn't cry, not now in front of her Papa. 'And I never do things in the right order, *sì*?'

'Like I said, it's a new age. We will have an heir sooner rather than later. That is good news. And the father?'

She looked away, unable to talk about Lucas and not show her true feelings. 'He's a good man. A wonderful man.'

'And…? Do you love him?'

Did she?

She felt emotions wash through her. What had started as a challenge had grown into so much more. He had taken her heart and made it his. He was stoic and steady and funny and sexy. More importantly, he believed in her. Made her feel as if she could conquer the world, and she had no doubt he would be a very good father once they'd worked things out.

There was something deep between them. Something more than friendship, more than anything she'd ever known before. It was painful and wonderful at the same time and she didn't want to think about a future without him.

So, yes, she loved him. Very much.

And that made everything a million times worse. She'd fallen in love and then walked away and her heart had shattered into so many pieces she knew she'd never fix it again.

A rogue tear spilled down her cheek. 'He won't be coming to live in the palace, although he will visit and be a part of our child's life. But I will bring this baby up in Isola Verde.'

'As Queen?'

She could do this. For her father, her family. For her baby and her country. She could be the person she'd always wanted to be. Yes. She could do this.

Barely able to move and yet shaking all over,

she pressed her lips to his forehead as his eyes drifted closed. 'If that is what you want, Papa. Then, yes, as Queen.'

Lucas was damned glad to see the back of Christmas Day.

Every time he saw the Christmas tree in the hospital foyer he thought about Gigi. When a mother brought in a sick baby he thought about Gigi and their child. The Princess was everywhere…in his head at least.

Then there'd been the stilted conversation with his parents during which he'd told them about the baby. In a gesture so typical of his family it was almost laughable, they'd sent over a formal contract for Giada to sign that guaranteed him access. That was all they'd said about the matter. No good luck wish or congratulations. No excitement or promises of knitting or babysitting.

And the ache in his chest had intensified and all the antacids in the world hadn't fixed it.

So last night he'd printed off the contract and now he was sitting in the doctors' mess, going through the legalese, feeling as if he was betraying Gigi in some way. Every way. But he had to make sure he got to watch his baby grow up. Hell, it was the only real family he'd ever have.

As he read, he had half an ear on the ever-present news channel on the TV on the wall.

Blah-blah. Blah. Isola Verde. Blah.

What? His head shot up and he stared at the TV. Isola Verde? Mentioned on the local news?

Did that mean…? Had Roberto died? But he'd thought their VIP patient was on the mend.

Backdropped by the Seattle General Hospital sign, Giada was reading from a script she held in her very steady hand. She looked…well, hell, she looked beautiful in a blue velvet coat that hid her bump, but he knew it was there. His heart, his whole body, hurt to see her and not touch her, not hold her in his arms, not kiss her.

God, these last few weeks had been torture. Once he'd thought he'd caught the scent of her perfume and had followed it up a hospital corridor looking for her before realising he was going mad. He'd ached to phone her, to talk to Dom, but Lucas had retreated, leaving them to pull together as the family she'd always wished they'd been. They wouldn't have wanted him there, but, hell, he'd strained for any information about the VIP patient and visitors.

Lucas watched as Gigi handled herself so serenely, scanning to see if there was any hint of heartbreak in her demeanour. No. Nothing. He smiled to himself. She wore her Royal demeanour well. He zoned in on her words…

'My father, King Roberto, is regrettably stepping down as King of Isola Verde. While his health is slowly improving, the surgery was to remove a brain tumour...' She paused—he imagined to let the gravity of that sink in. 'He needs time to rest. He wishes to announce that I, Giada Francesca Vittoria Baresi, will ascend the throne...'

What the hell? Lucas's heart bumped and jolted. Not Dom? What was happening?

He jumped up and paced the room. She was going to be Queen. Their child was going to be heir to the throne? What, then, for him? For their child?

He stopped pacing. She would make sure he saw their child grow up. In that palace.

His optimism waned. Access maybe once or twice a year. He'd sit on the sidelines and watch Giada rule and marry and have more children. See another man fall in love with her, watch her eyes fill with love for another guy. Meanwhile, he'd talk to her through lawyers and they'd both wear that damned mask of indifference when inside his heart would be crumbling.

He rubbed his chest. He would not be able to bear watching her fall for someone else, or see another man touch her.

He loved her. He looked around the room. Sure, he was in Seattle and, sure, he'd spent a good part of his life securing this job he loved. But was this it? For the rest of his life? Lonely? Missing her? Traversing the globe twice a year to catch a glimpse of a family he ached to be part of?

He looked at the papers, tore them into tiny pieces and threw them in the bin. There had to be another way.

He was going to make sure there was.

A new year. A new beginning. And what a year she was going to have!

Giada opened the curtains and looked out over the gardens towards the woods and beyond, to the lake. Dappled sunshine and the beat of horse hooves reminded her that her father would soon be home. Things had healed so much between them and she couldn't wait to have him back home and to help him recuperate.

She stretched out her arms, breathing in the cooler Mediterranean air and oh! A funny little feeling in her belly. Like butterfly wings. Not nervous, more…

Oh! A smile wound through her and she closed her eyes, cupping her growing bump. He was kicking. Her little Prince…or Princess…was turning and tumbling. 'Hey, little one. Hello.'

Her throat closed over and she couldn't say much then, apart from, 'Mummy loves you. Daddy does too. I just wish… No. Daddy loves you very much.'

No more wishing. It was the first day of the

year. She needed to put all that behind her as best she could. There was still a shadow on her heart that would always be Lucas-shaped but she had to concentrate on herself, this pregnancy and her coronation plans.

Her phone rang. Maria. 'Your Highness, there's a visitor for you.'

'It's New Year's Day. Can you ask them to come back tomorrow?' She had some serious baby shopping to do and a nursery to plan. 'Don't I get even one day off? I'm starting to rethink this whole Queen business.' Of course she wasn't, and Maria knew that.

'I think you might want to come down for this.'

'Why? What can possibly be more important than choosing cute baby clothes?' She'd told her assistant about her pregnancy. The only one still out of the loop was her brother.

Maria laughed. 'He says to tell you Captain Sensible's gone into retirement. But Captain Spontaneous would very much like to see you.'

Lucas!

Her heart tumbled and turned, just like their baby, and she ran to the top of the grand staircase. There he was in the hall, shimmering in the light of the dome, tall and handsome and beautiful and serious.

'Hello.' She felt nervous, just like the time she'd

sneaked into his suite. Was he here to talk? To hit her with a lawsuit? To…?

He captured her gaze. 'Giada.'

Not Gigi. That was important. She descended the stairs on shaking legs. 'Lucas. Nice of you to visit.'

He fisted his hands, didn't kiss her cheek. 'I need to tell you something.'

'Go right ahead.'

'I told my parents about the baby.'

That was a step forward. 'Good.'

He shook his head. 'Not so good. They advised me to serve you with papers to ensure I was allowed access.'

That was why he was here? Her stomach felt as if it was tumbling to her feet. 'You could have emailed them. Saved yourself the journey.'

'I… I needed to see you. To talk to you. Because that's the way to do these things, right? To communicate face to face.' He reached out and stroked her cheek with his fingertips. 'I don't want sporadic access to my child. I want more than that.'

'You want full custody?' Her heart jerked and she stepped out of his reach. '*Dio*, Lucas… please…no. I don't want to fight.'

I love you.

How would he react if she just said it? Was

honest with him instead of hiding behind pretence?

'Yes…' He cleared his throat and straightened. 'Joint custody. I want us to be a family, Gigi. I want my Gigi back. Not the one who walked away. I want the one who is real and honest and kisses like an angel.'

'You want… But you do know I'm going to be Queen? I can't move to Seattle.' There it was. The real problem.

But he smiled. And, God, it was beautiful. 'I know. I don't care where we live. Honestly. I'm sure I could get used to all this, given a chance. I hope. I'll try. I want to try. I spent too long fighting the idea. I blocked everything else. I didn't want to fall for you and then for you to walk away.'

Like his parents had. Love, in his experience, was conditional. 'I walked away.'

'Yes.'

'Oh, Lucas.' She'd done exactly what he'd thought she would do, the worst thing she could have done. She'd made her love conditional on him living here and when she'd thought he couldn't do that she'd walked away. 'I tried hard not to let you into my heart. I thought I could tease you and have fun but then it got serious and I got scared because the feelings I had were so intense. I didn't want to believe…'

'I know.' He held out his hand and she took it. 'I know why you did it. I understand, Gigi. You've been treated badly in the past, but you don't have to put on a brave face with me. Ever.'

He knew her better than she knew herself. And she knew him well too. 'You could work at the hospital. I think that's important. You'd be grumpy otherwise. Lucas, I—'

'I love you.'

She didn't know who said it first. Who took the first step, who leaned in first. But his lips touched hers. And then she was wrapped in his arms, the only place she wanted to be. Her home. Her Lucas.

She pulled away but kept hold of him. 'Captain Spontaneous?'

'Hmm.' He nuzzled her hair and laughed. 'Sensible has been sent into exile.'

'Good.' Now it was her turn to clear her throat. 'You know a queen should probably be married, *sì*?'

His eyebrows rose. 'Is this…? Giada Francesca Vittoria Baresi, is this a proposal?'

She laughed because, yes, it probably was. 'Papa said I always do things the wrong way round. But when you asked me you didn't mean it. So now it's my turn. And I *do* mean it. Dr Lucas Beaufort, will you marry me?'

'*Sì, bella* Gigi.' He kissed her again and again,

his hand sliding round to her abdomen. His eyes widened and he jerked back. 'Is that? Did the baby just…?'

'Yes.' She put his hand back again. 'He or she is very happy.'

'So am I.' Then he got serious. 'I really think we need to tell Domenico.'

'We should call him. He'll be thrilled.'

Lucas grimaced and ran fingers through his hair. 'He'll kill me.'

She waved her hand. 'You can't kill the Queen's husband. He'll have his head chopped off. Let's call him…in a few minutes. I have Royal business to attend to first. The Queen would like to kiss her Consort.'

And then she did.

For a very long time.

EPILOGUE

One year later...

'IT'S MY TURN for cuddles.' Roberto Baresi took his granddaughter from Gigi's aching arms and planted a big kiss on baby Chiara Alessia Giada Beaufort-Baresi's chubby cheek. 'Who's a lovely girl, then?'

'Who is he and what has he done with my father?' Dom whispered once their father was out of earshot over the other side of the room. They were all crammed into the antechamber on the second floor of the palace. The noise was reaching fever pitch inside, matching the crowds down below.

Giada made a feeble attempt to hush her inside guests. 'Thank you for coming. All of you. It's been a very special Christmas and…er… coronation…' Because why have one celebration when you can have two? 'I'm so glad we got to share it all with you. Thank you for everything. Now drink!'

Gigi laughed as she looked at the smiling faces, her heart so full of love and joy and hope. Domenico had come over from Seattle with Emilia, married now and settled together. After Gigi's announcement, the news had broken about his true identity and for a few weeks there'd been a buzz, but it had all died down. They were very happy, she could see. Still competing, still working, still very good friends.

He'd forgiven both her and Lucas for their relationship…but it had taken a few weeks for their happy equilibrium to right itself.

Dom had brought Max Granger and Ayanna Franklin over for the holidays. They'd finally admitted they were an item and Ayanna was happily planning their wedding. More fun!

Logan had come too…back to see his old boss, bringing his son, little Jamie, and his wife Kat, the nurse who'd first seen Giada after the accident. And they'd shared the happy news that they would soon be adopting. Another baby.

Gigi put down her champagne glass and smoothed her dress. 'Right, how do I look?'

'Very regal.' Emilia straightened Gigi's purple sash. 'Oh, your crown's a bit crooked.'

'Story of my life.' Gigi laughed as she put her hands onto the precious crystals and diamonds and tried to fix it.

'Wait…let me.' Lucas stepped in front of her

and her heart leapt as it always did. He pressed a kiss to her cheek then did something to her crown and it felt straight and right. He slipped his hand into hers. 'I love you, Queen Gigi.'

Oh, he did, she was utterly and totally convinced of that. And he couldn't be a better father. Although the hospital work was mostly what was keeping him sane.

'Ma'am. It's time.' The footman drew back the heavy velvet drapes and the sound from the crowd intensified.

'Oh, wait… Chiara… I'd better take her. Come on, Lucas. It's showtime.'

'I prefer bedtime, but there it is,' he whispered against her throat. And she felt the thrill of anticipation shiver through her. There was so much love. She was so damned lucky.

Then they stepped out onto the balcony and a roar erupted from the crowd. Giada waved with her baby-free hand and knew that happiness radiated from her. Her heart was full.

She had her family, her country, her baby. And her husband by her side. For ever.

* * * * *

*Welcome to the Royal Christmas
at Seattle General quartet!*

Falling for the Secret Prince
by Alison Roberts

Neurosurgeon's Christmas to Remember
by Traci Douglass

The Bodyguard's Christmas Proposal
by Charlotte Hawkes

The Princess's Christmas Baby
by Louisa George

All available now!